BLOOD GOLD

THE WANDERER SERIES
BOOK TWO

D1316878

G. MICHAEL HOPF

DEDICATION

TO THOSE WHO WENT BEFORE US. THEIR
HARD WORK AND SACRIFICE LAID THE
FOUNDATION FOR OUR GREAT REPUBLIC.

"Happiness resides not in possessions, and not in gold, happiness dwells in the soul."

- Democritus

PROLOGUE

"Fast is fine, but accuracy is everything." – Wyatt Earp

DODGE CITY, KANSAS

SEPTEMBER 15, 1876

Marshal Larry Deger put his hands on his hips, scrunched his face and growled, "Listen here. This is your last chance. I'm a fair man, but in a matter of days you've managed to draw down on a man who was only holding a cane, and brawled with three cowboys, leaving one with a broken arm."

"To be fair, Marshal, I was justified in both incidents," John replied. "And that wasn't really a cane, it was a sword, and he intended on using it."

"Last chance," Deger said, adjusting his gun belt around his rotund midsection. Deger was a massive man, weighing over three hundred pounds. John was astonished how quickly he could move for a man of his size.

A gunshot rang out from inside the rowdy Longhorn Saloon, causing both men to turn their heads.

"I think I need to go in," John said.

"You hear me, last chance," Deger said.

John was appreciative of Deger giving him another and final chance to prove he was meant to be a lawman. He'd traveled a long way and happened into the job after both Morgan and Wyatt Earp had resigned to go find their fortunes in Deadwood. John told himself the timing was fate, but for Marshal Deger, it was more about filling the spot, and John happened to be there.

The only issue John had run into while on the job was his temper, or his lack of control of it. In a matter of days, he'd gotten himself into a bit of trouble, and trouble was something Deger wanted to avoid, especially any that had to do with himself or his office. John turned to head inside to confront the man shooting, but Deger stopped him. "Hold on. I'm not sure this is such a good idea."

Facing Deger once more, John pleaded, "Marshal, I've got this. You can trust me."

"Just go in, ask him to turn over his firearms, and leave it at that. Don't escalate this. Do you understand me?" Deger warned.

"Yes, sir," John said, nodding.

"And, Nichols, this is your last chance. If this goes sideways, I'm taking your badge."

"I heard you, Marshal. No need to worry. I have this," John said, turned and pushed his way through the swinging doors and entered the saloon. All eyes shifted from the drunken and rowdy man to John. The piano stopped playing, and the chatter turned to whispers.

"You all listen, and listen good. I'm the biggest and most ornery son of a bitch you'll ever come up against," the belligerent man barked, stepping up to a man seated playing poker and yelling in his face. The rowdy man was a cowboy from Texas and had just arrived on a cattle run. He was lean and stood average height; his tanned face was covered with a thick scruffy beard.

"Thomas, just sit your ass down," the man's friend said from the bar, a full glass of whiskey in his hand.

"Go to hell, Francis," Thomas spat. He looked around at the quiet faces and blared, "See, you all listened and shut your damn mouths."

John approached Thomas, stopping six feet from him. "I'm gonna have to ask you to turn in your guns."

Thomas looked up and began to laugh heartily. He turned to Francis and continued to chuckle. He looked back at John and asked, "Who the hell are you?"

"I'm Assistant Marshal Nichols. Now this is what's going to happen. You have two choices, well, maybe three, but let's start with the first two—" John said but was interrupted.

"Go to hell!" Thomas roared. In his right hand he clenched a Colt, and in his left a bottle of whiskey.

"First choice, you hand me your guns, all of them. If you do, you can go back to enjoying your evening. The second choice is you force me to disarm you, and, well, let's just say that you'll get hurt and you'll spend the night in jail."

Thomas cut his eyes and asked, "What's the third choice?"

"It's my least favorite, and I daresay it will be yours too," John replied, slowly pulling his right hand back towards his holstered Colt.

"I should just shoot you. You're nothin' but a dumb son of a bitch," Thomas snapped in anger.

"The third choice is if you attempt to point your firearm with the intent to do me or anyone in this

3

establishment harm, I'll kill you right where you stand," John said sternly.

"Kill! You're gonna draw your gun faster than I can raise mine? Son, you're as dumb as those cattle we rustle," Thomas said mockingly.

Deger entered the saloon when he heard John give his third option, but declined to get involved. He stepped to the side, gingerly placed his right hand on the back strap of his holstered Number 3 Model Remington revolver, and waited, hoping John kept his word and didn't escalate the situation. Deger was a fair man, and if the other man wanted a fight, he had no problem with any of his men defending themselves. What caused his consternation was John's way of handling things.

"We expect everyone in Dodge City to enjoy themselves, but we also expect they follow our laws," John said.

"Laws, to hell with your laws!" Thomas yelled. He took a step towards John, but stopped when he saw John's gaze narrow and his body tense. His hesitation soon waned as the alcohol he'd been swigging since earlier in the day removed any logical sense. His grip tightened on the Colt in his hand, and he edged it up an inch.

"Stay where you are, and place your gun on the table now," John warned. He cut his eyes to Francis and added, "And don't think that I don't see you too."

Francis put his glass down and squared off in John's direction.

Seeing Francis' move in support, Thomas grew more

confident. "Listen here, Assistant Marshal, I won't be giving you my gun, nor will I do as you say. I've been out running cattle for weeks, I'm tired, and I plan on having a hell of a good time."

"Like I said, we want you cowboys to enjoy yourselves, but do so respecting the laws and ways of our town," John said coolly.

"I will do whatever I want, including taking a few more steps towards you," Thomas barked.

"Don't do it," John warned.

Thomas didn't listen. He shuffled a few feet, but when he went to take another step, John cleared the distance, grabbed the pistol from his hand, drew his own, and smashed the butt of the Colt on top of his head. Thomas' eyes rolled back into his head as he dropped to the dusty floor, unconscious.

Seeing his friend get knocked out, Francis made his move.

John caught sight of him and said, "Don't think about it. I'll drop you."

Francis didn't listen. He reached across his body and pulled his pistol.

Having the advantage, John casually turned, cocked the Colt and squeezed the trigger. The bullet roared from the muzzle and struck Francis squarely in the chest.

Francis stepped back and into the bar. He looked down at the hole in his chest and began to cough up blood. He lifted his gaze towards John and mumbled, "You shot me."

"I told you not to do it," John said.

Francis coughed up even more blood, said something unintelligible, and dropped to the floor, dead.

"Shit," John said, knowing Deger would be angry.

Thomas opened his eyes, pulled a long sheath knife from his boot and swung at John, barely missing him.

John stepped aside and stared at Thomas as he kept swinging.

"Are you done yet?" John asked.

"I'll kill you, you son of a bitch," Thomas groaned.

Impatient, John kicked the knife from his hand, then kicked Thomas in the jaw, again knocking him out.

With one man dead and the other incapacitated, the saloon broke out into cheers and applause. The bartender hollered, "Assistant Marshal Nichols, drinks on the house when you want them."

John tipped his hat to the bartender and looked at the scene. Blood pooled around Francis' body, and Thomas was sprawled out on the floor, unconscious.

Deger walked up beside him and said, "You were doing good until you gave him that third option. Hell, even your second option was a bit too antagonistic. You just couldn't ask for their guns and be done with it? You had to make it a show of sorts. I don't know why you do that, but I can say that style of law enforcement won't work in Dodge City."

"Marshal, did you see what happened? That man over there drew on me. I was justified. And his friend on the floor, he came at me. I could have easily shot him dead and would have been right to do so, but I didn't, and the reason why—'cause I knew you'd prefer I not kill anyone."

"You don't get it, Nichols. It's your tone; you don't try to reason with them, you challenge them. Of course cock-strong cowboys are gonna get riled up when they've been challenged."

"These men don't take to authority, that's all," John said defensively.

Deger shook his head and said, "You're not a good fit for this line of work. You have too much…"

John waited for Deger to finish the thought, but he didn't. He only looked around and shook his head.

"Too much what?"

"Anger, too much anger. Nichols, you're one of the angriest people I've ever met, and I think you enjoy getting into fights," Deger said.

"I won't lie that I don't mind a good fight, but I don't start these things, these people do. I'm merely defending myself," John said.

"Enough talk. Look at this mess I have to deal with, and now I have to go talk to their boss and explain."

"I'll try even harder next time," John said.

Deger turned and faced John. "There won't be a next time. You're done. Give me your badge." Deger held out his open hand.

John looked down at Deger's hand, shocked he was being fired. "Oh, c'mon, Marshal, I was defending myself."

"You're just not a good fit. Maybe you should have joined Wyatt and Morgan and gone to Deadwood. Who knows, maybe your calling is in gold prospecting."

"Marshal, give me another chance," John urged.

"Give me your badge…now," Deger ordered.

John's temper flared, but he kept it under control. He ripped the badge from his vest and slapped it into Deger's hand. "You're making a mistake."

"Nichols, you're a good man, but I think you're meant for something else."

John turned and exited the saloon. A cool breeze swept over him, and the sounds of the town hit his ears. He'd come into town filled with the promise of a new life, but that was now over. Deger's comment about Deadwood popped into his head. Maybe he should go and see what opportunities were available. Having fulfilled his promise to his murdered wife and daughter by finding their killers, he'd imagined Dodge City would be a new chapter. He'd just never thought it would be so short lived.

"Good shootin' in there," a man said as he exited the saloon and walked up to John.

John looked at the unfamiliar man and said, "Thanks."

"Did I see what I think I saw?" the man asked.

John leaned back and got a good look at the man. He was finely dressed in a tailored wool suit, and his thin mustache was perfectly trimmed. "What do you want?"

"Mr. Nichols, my name is Horatio Rothman. My son and I are on our way to Deadwood to see about a gold claim. We're unfamiliar with the subtleties of these towns and are in need of a man like you."

"Like what?"

"A man who can handle himself. Listen, Mr. Nichols, we need protection, and I believe you're the man for the job."

"Wait, how do you know my name?"

"I happened to see you gun down that man the other day. I asked about you and was informed you were the assistant marshal."

"Well, I'm not interested," John said and stepped away.

"I'll pay you ten thousand dollars to take me and my son to Deadwood and provide protection for the next couple of months while we get set up to work our claim."

Shocked by the amount, John instantly became interested. "Ten thousand?"

"In cash or gold, whichever you prefer," Horatio said as he pulled a pipe from his jacket pocket and stuck it between his teeth.

"Payment up front," John said.

"I'm a generous man, not a fool, Mr. Nichols. I'll pay you three thousand when we leave, another three when we arrive in Deadwood and the balance once we've established ourselves in the area and gotten our claim up and running."

John thought. Here he was losing one opportunity, and suddenly another made itself available. This clearly was providence.

Deger exited the saloon, looked at John and said, "If you're waiting to see if I've changed my mind, the answer is no."

"I wasn't waiting here for you. I was talking to Mr.

Rothman."

"Hmm," Deger said and walked off.

John watched Deger walk away. He was happy to be done with him. "Stupid man," John said above a whisper.

"What was that?" Horatio asked.

"It's nothing, but I have a sinking suspicion the marshal will end up in a pine box before too long."

"Because he's careless?" Horatio asked.

"No, because he's fat. Have you ever seen a man that large before?" John said, referring to Deger's large size.

Horatio dismissed the petty talk and asked, "Do we have a deal?"

"Mr. Rothman, we do," John said confidently.

"Good, meet me and my son at the Kansan Hotel for breakfast. We'll give you all the details and get you paid."

"Paid?"

"Why, yes, Mr. Nichols, I said I'd pay you three thousand when we leave, so get your affairs in order and pack your things. We leave for Deadwood in the morning."

CHAPTER ONE

"All the gold which is under or upon the earth is not enough to give in exchange for virtue." – Plato

TWENTY-THREE MILES SOUTH OF DEADWOOD, DAKOTA TERRITORY

SEPTEMBER 24, 1876

The ride from Dodge City was taking longer than John liked, but there wasn't a thing he could do. Horatio, his son, William, and the wagon full of goods were making what should be a three- to four-day ride into a slow and grinding ten-day trek.

"Let's hold up here for the night," Horatio ordered the driver of the wagon.

The driver, Hans, a German immigrant from New York and longtime associate of Horatio's, pulled on the reins of the horse team. "Sir, we're close, maybe another four to six hours."

Horatio looked at William, who showed the fatigue on his face, and said, "We're tired. Let's call it a night; we'll rise early and set out." He slowly dismounted and walked his horse to a clearing off the road.

John, who was riding ahead, heard Horatio's command and immediately turned around. "We're almost there, and I for one could use a good bed and a hot bath," John said to Horatio, watching him unpack his saddlebags.

William trotted over to his father and said, "Father, John is right. Let's continue on. I too could use a hot bath." William looked at John and gave him a nod. He was a tall and slender man, towering over six feet five, and in the saddle of a horse, he looked like a rigid stick that could snap at any moment.

"William, while I appreciate your enthusiasm, we'll camp here tonight. My thighs hurt, and to be quite honest, I'm exhausted and my body really aches," Horatio replied.

John opened his mouth to speak, but Horatio cut him off. "I'm sure John would agree that it's getting dark soon, and our last couple of hours of the ride would have us doing so in the dark. That isn't entirely safe due to the road agents that are known to prey upon travelers just outside Deadwood. And we all read what happened to Marshal Brown." This was a reference to the first marshal of Deadwood, who had been gunned down a little over a month ago while traveling back to Deadwood from Crook City.

John was familiar with road agents, or bandits, but Deadwood had gotten a reputation for them beyond other towns or areas. Being that Deadwood itself was an illegal settlement, being established in the middle of Lakota Territory and in clear violation of the Treaty of Fort Laramie, the town of Deadwood was rampant with crime, and road agents were prevalent on many roads and trails that led to and from the town.

Although he was willing to take the risk, John was

being paid to provide protection, and Horatio had a point. He dismounted Molly and said, "I'll take first shift."

William shrugged his shoulders and also dismounted his horse. He walked it over to where John was tying up Molly and said, "You know it's okay to challenge my father. He trusts you."

"Your father is right. We need to be wary of road agents just outside town, and traveling at night is too risky."

"But you would keep us safe," William said as he loosened the belly strap on his saddle and removed it from his horse's back.

"I'm not sure what you heard about me, but there's one thing I can't do, and that's see in the dark. Tonight we'll rest, and at first light we'll set out. We should reach Deadwood by midday." John removed the saddle from Molly and brought it over to the clearing where Horatio was setting up a campsite.

William followed him and placed his saddle next to John's. "Um, if you don't mind me asking. How was the war?"

John gave him a cross look and said, "I do mind you asking."

"I'm not trying to offend. I'm just curious. Father insisted I finish my schooling. He said if I was going to go, I should be an officer."

"I'll say this, you're lucky you didn't go," John said.

"On the contrary, I'm envious. I mean, even though you fought for the rebellion, I wish I had been there to do my duty," William said, standing tall and lifting his chest.

John shook his head, removed his bedroll, and spread it out.

"The glory and honor of fighting for a cause, even your cause, must have made you proud."

Unable to hold back his honest thoughts, John turned and growled, "You know what glory and honor I saw after four years of fighting?"

William stared at John, his face frozen in a look of shock.

"I came back to find my home burned to the ground and my family murdered by Union soldiers. All the War of Northern Aggression gave me was death, despair and nightmares. While you Yankees might have won, and you may feel there's glory in that victory, I can tell you there isn't for the men who didn't return or the ones who did but with their bodies and minds shattered. No, the idea of glory is for those timid souls who don't know the horrors of the battlefield."

William turned ashen.

Feet away, Horatio sat stunned as he overheard John's diatribe.

Hans, a Union veteran who had fought with the Eighth New York Volunteer Infantry Regiment, or what the men in the unit called the First New York German Rifles, chuckled at John's comment. Like John, he was intimately familiar with the carnage of war.

Horatio shot Hans a look but withheld from reprimanding him for his obvious disdain towards

William.

"I, ah, well, I'm sure not all of those who fought feel that way," William countered John.

"Then I daresay they weren't on the front lines," John fired back.

"I'll have you know my uncle—" William began to say but was interrupted by Horatio.

"Gentlemen, I find your conversation becoming a bore. Let's set up camp and relax," Horatio said, pointing towards the level ground that he proposed for the campsite.

"But, Father, John here—" William rebutted.

"William, do as I say. In fact, go gather some wood for the fire," Horatio ordered.

William sneered at his father then gave John a scowl.

"Listen to your father," John said.

"This conversation isn't over," William said and marched off to fetch wood.

Hans walked up alongside John and whispered, "Don't be too hard on the boy. His father and mother have kept him sheltered all his life. If he'd seen what we'd seen, he would have wet his trousers."

"If what I said was too rough, he's got a rude awakening for what he's about to experience in Deadwood."

DEADWOOD, DAKOTA TERRITORY

Sven Jacobsen threw open the tent flap and stood staring at his wife, Anna.

"What is it?" she asked with concern after seeing his red face and flaring nostrils.

"He lied!" Sven roared.

Anna, busy mending a shirt, dropped what she was doing and asked, "Lied? Who?"

"Jimmy O'Riodian, that's who. I'll kill him, I will," Sven said, coming into the tent. He began to dig through his belongings.

"What are you looking for?" she asked.

He pulled out an old 1861 Navy Colt and wiped off the dust and grime that covered it.

"Sven, what are you planning to do?" she asked, coming to his side and placing her arms around him.

"Leave me be, woman. This is a man's business," Sven said as he began to search again. "Where is the powder and balls?"

"I don't know what you mean," Anna replied, her voice cracking with fear.

He shoved her away in anger and growled, "Leave me be!"

"You're scaring me," she said, tears welling in her blue eyes.

Sven found what he was looking for, pulled out a small wooden box and opened it. Inside he found a dozen thirty-six-caliber round balls, a pile of percussion caps, and a small black powder flask. He half-cocked the pistol, freeing up the cylinder to move, poured powder into all six chambers, laid a ball on top of the first chamber, then rotated it directly underneath the loading plunger and pulled the loading lever down until the ball was seated tightly in the chamber. He repeated this five more times. With the pistol loaded, he picked up a percussion cap, but dropped it, as his hands were slightly trembling with pure rage. He took a deep breath to calm himself and tried again. He placed the percussion cap on a nipple and rotated the cylinder until each nipple had a cap on it. With the pistol now ready to be fired, he stood and shoved it in the waistband of his trousers and marched out of the tent, leaving Anna cowering in the corner in fear.

Sven and Anna had immigrated to Minnesota from Sweden with hopes of opening a shop selling wares, but when news of the Black Hills gold rush came, Sven packed them up and moved directly to Deadwood. When they arrived, they found no claims to be had; that was until Sven met a man by the name of Abraham Saul. Abraham had a claim that encompassed two hundred feet along the banks of Deadwood Creek and told Sven he needed to sell it quickly due to a family emergency back in Chicago. After a prolonged back and forth, Sven told Abraham he needed to consult Anna as well as reconnoiter the claim. Abraham told him there was no time to see the claim, he was selling it within the hour. Sven managed to convince Abraham to at least allow him to talk to his wife. Abraham agreed. However, upon Sven's return to the Cricket Saloon, he discovered Abraham had sold the claim to a man by the name of Jimmy O'Riodian, a bouncer who worked for Liam Prince, the owner of the Cricket and a man whose reputation preceded him. Despondent that he had lost out on getting a claim, Sven turned to leave but not before Jimmy offered to sell it; however, he wanted an additional ten percent above the price Abraham had sold it to him for. Not willing to lose it again, Sven took the deal, paid Jimmy, and secured his claim.

The first week at his claim, Sven worked hard, but there was no gold to be found. By the end of week three, Sven had determined the claim was played out and there was no gold and he had been duped. After spending his family's life savings on a bogus claim, Sven was now hell-bent on seeking justice but in a town that knew none.

Sven pushed his way through the bustling crowds on Main Street until he was standing in front of the Cricket. Howls and cheers of merriment came from the establishment; it didn't matter what time of day, there always seemed to be something happening there. He touched the back strap of his pistol and paused for a moment. Doubts began to surface. *Am I truly prepared to kill a man for the claim? Can I? Or is the pistol merely a tool to threaten or show how serious I am?* Thoughts of Anna being left poor and destitute because of his rush to find fortune plagued him. He needed to get his money back, there was no other choice, and the pistol would help him make his point. He pressed his eyes closed and mumbled a prayer in Swedish. Before he could open his eyes, someone called his name.

"Sven, what in the hell are you doing standing there looking like a man on a mission?" Jimmy called out from the front deck of the Cricket.

Sven opened his eyes to see the man he'd come to

see. "It's played out. The damn claim is played out!"

Jimmy cocked his head and said, "I'm not sure what you're talking about."

Sven rushed forward, his body rigid with rage; he stopped inches from Jimmy's face and hollered, "I want my money back!"

Jimmy stiffened and with a subtle but tough tone said, "Now, Sven, I'm not sure how you square heads handle business where you come from, but coming up on a man and yelling accusations and demands while your hand is on a pistol will get you shot here."

With the pistol now mentioned, Sven decided to pull it. Holding it tightly in his right hand, he raged, "Give me my money back!"

Jimmy, who had been leaning against a railing, stood and leaned close to Sven, so much he could feel his hot breath. "I'm going to give you a bit of advice here. If you pull a weapon on a man, you best use it right away."

"What in the hell is going on?" Liam Prince hollered as he exited the Cricket. Seeing the tension between both men, he stepped in between them. "Sven, I see you came here to do some negotiating, but I can tell ya, I wouldn't do that type with Jimmy and especially with that antique you have there."

"Your man sold me a bogus claim. It's played out, Liam, the claim is played out. There's no gold there!" Sven yelled.

Liam placed his hand on Sven's shoulder and said calmly, "How about you put that thing away and come into the bar where we can talk over a glass of whiskey like civilized men?"

"I want my money back!" Sven replied, tearing his gaze from Jimmy and putting it on Liam.

"I understand you have a disagreement, but let's work this out. So come inside. Drinks are on me. We can all discuss this without bloodshed," Liam said.

Jimmy stood, his hard stare never leaving Sven's face.

Liam shoved Jimmy and said, "Right, Jimmy, we'll discuss this like civilized men."

"Yes, boss," Jimmy answered and strutted inside with the other two following.

***

"Liam, the claim is bogus. I've been working it about three weeks now. There's no gold," Sven said, his thick Swedish accent making it tough for Liam to understand him.

"Slow down and pronounce your words," Liam barked.

"I sold you that claim fair and square. If you didn't reconnoiter it beforehand, that's not my business," Jimmy fired back.

"I didn't have time!" Sven countered.

"Then whose fault is that?" Jimmy snarked.

Several men close by began to listen to the conversation. Seeing them, Liam barked, "Mind your own business." He turned to Sven and Jimmy and said, "Let's take this to my office in the back."

Sven took a seat in a chair directly in front of Liam's

desk. Liam sat behind his desk, with Jimmy standing to Liam's right, his back pressed against the uneven wall. The glow of several oil lamps cast an orange hue across the small room.

"Three weeks is not enough time to truly assess a claim, and might I add, do you know what you're doing?" Liam asked.

Sven shot back, "I do."

"Bullshit, you square heads don't know shit about mining," Jimmy mocked.

"You shut your mouth, you...you scam artist," Sven yelled, his index finger pointed firmly at Jimmy.

"Sven, shut up. Enough of the accusations!" Liam barked as he slammed his fist against his desk. "You came to camp when?"

"Four weeks ago," Sven answered.

"And did you mine for gold somewhere else?" Liam asked.

"No."

"Have you ever mined for gold anywhere before?" Liam asked.

Sheepishly Sven answered, "No, but—"

"Then how do you know there's not gold there? Maybe Jimmy is right. You don't know what you're doing," Liam suggested.

"I know how to read and—"

"Liam, I've had enough of this. He bought the claim fair and square, you were there, and now 'cause he doesn't know what he's doing, he wants to get his money back," Jimmy said.

"Why don't you just resell it?" Liam asked.

"'Cause any man who knows mining will know that claim is played out. There's no gold on it," Sven replied. He took a deep breath and snapped, "If I don't get my money back, I'm going out there and telling everyone you're selling bogus claims. I'll make sure the entire camp knows."

Liam's reasonable tone shifted. "You listen here, you damn square head. You go out there and slander my name, I'll have you gutted within the hour and your remains fed to the hogs."

"Liam, I'm looking for justice here; you're either with me or against me," Sven warned and stood up.

Liam once again slammed his fist down. "Sit your ass down!"

Seeing Liam's temper truly flare, Sven did as he said.

Taking a deep breath, Liam said calmly, "I'm going to mediate this, and both of you are going to do what I say or I'll have you both fed to the hogs."

Neither man spoke.

"Do you understand?" Liam asked.

Jimmy and Sven nodded.

"Jimmy is going to go out with you to the claim in the morning to help. He has real experience as a miner. He has it in his blood. His father was in California during the gold-rush days of the late forties. He will spend the next week with you, ensuring you know how to mine gold properly—"

"But, Liam," Jimmy chimed in.

Liam pointed his finger and snarled, "Shut your

mouth and listen."

Jimmy nodded.

"He will help you, and if after a good honest week of mining, you find no gold, I will buy that claim from you."

"You will?" Sven asked.

"You have my word. Reason why is I know that claim is good 'cause Abraham was coming into the Cricket almost nightly and spending his finds. There's gold there; you just don't know what you're doing," Liam said, looking at both men. "Now do we have a deal?"

Jimmy once more nodded.

"Yes," Sven answered.

"Good. Now get your ass out of my office, Sven. Feel free to get a whiskey on the house before you leave."

Sven promptly left the office, closing the door behind him.

"Liam, what in the hell?" Jimmy asked, a look of confusion on his face.

"Tomorrow you're going to take that square head piece of shit out to his claim—"

"But, Liam, you and I both know that claim is played out. We'll never find gold there," Jimmy said, interrupting Liam.

A look of irritation spread across Liam's face. "Can you just keep your mouth shut so I can explain the plan?"

"Yes, boss."

"Good. Take the square head out to his claim and make it look like an accident, and while you're at it, find Saul. I don't need that Jew bastard talking either."

"What about the wife?" Jimmy asked, referring to

Anna.

"Let me handle that," Liam replied.

CHAPTER TWO

"Delay is preferable to error." – Thomas Jefferson

TWENTY-THREE MILES SOUTH OF DEADWOOD, DAKOTA TERRITORY

SEPTEMBER 25, 1876

John woke to find Hans leaning against the wagon, smoking a pipe. The fire was still ablaze, providing warmth for the chilly morning, but what excited John the most was the sight of the metal pot suspended over it by an iron rod and hook. He knew inside a blend of ground coffee and chicory awaited him. He slipped on his boots and rose to go find the closest shrub to relieve himself. When he returned, he found William sitting up.

"Good morning," William said in a chipper tone.

"Mornin'," John answered as he beelined it for the coffee.

"Do you mind pouring me a cup too?" William asked, getting to his feet. He stretched and started to scratch his head.

"Sure," John said. He looked over at Hans and asked, "You need a cup?"

"I'm good, my friend, thank you," Hans replied.

John poured the coffees and handed one to William. The two chatted and shared small talk until William was curious why his father wasn't rising yet. "Father, it's time to wake."

No response.

William walked over and tapped his father's leg. "Time to wake."

Horatio grunted and rolled onto his back.

When William saw his splotchy red face and glossy eyes, he asked, "Father, are you well?"

"No, no, I'm not. I feel horrible," Horatio answered.

William knelt and pulled the wool blanket back, exposing a rash on Horatio's neck and upper chest.

Horatio quickly pulled the blanket back up to cover his shivering body. "I'm freezing."

John stepped over and looked down. "Does he have a fever?"

William stood and replied, "He does, I'm afraid. What should we do?"

John pulled William away from Horatio so he couldn't overhear. He leaned in and whispered, "Was that a rash I saw?"

"Yes," William answered.

"Pox?" John asked.

"Not sure," William replied.

Needing to know, John went to Horatio's side, quickly lowered the blanket, took a look, and covered him up again. After surviving a smallpox outbreak when he was a teenager, he was familiar with the rash, and it only took him a couple of seconds to know that was what Horatio had. He took William by the arm and escorted him away so they could have a conversation.

"Did you see something else?" William asked, a look

of concern on his childlike face.

"He's got the pox," John said flatly.

"What do we do?" William asked, his voice cracking with emotion.

"We toss him in the wagon *pronto*, as you Americans say. Get him to a doc in Deadwood," Hans said, puffing on his pipe.

"He's right. We need to get him into town. There's nothing we can do for him here," John said. He looked over at Hans and continued, "Clear a spot in the back of the wagon. If we need to leave some things, do so."

Hans nodded and went to work.

John immediately went to gather his things.

William followed him around like a duckling chases his mother until John stopped him. "What are you doing? Get your stuff together. We're leaving right away."

"Will he die?" William asked.

Seeing the raw emotion in William's face, John thought before he merely blurted out something. "You want the straight truth?"

"Of course," William answered.

"He could, so let's hurry."

DEADWOOD CREEK, FIVE MILES OUTSIDE DEADWOOD, DAKOTA TERRITORY

Sven was skeptical of them finding anything, but he'd made a deal with Liam, and he was going to honor his word.

The entire ride out to the claim, Jimmy groaned and

complained, often making passive-aggressive comments.

"First thing I need you to do is show me where and how you were prospecting," Jimmy said.

Sven pointed to the creek and said, "I've been shoveling from the center of the creek, placing it into the bucket, and sifting from there."

Jimmy shook his head and mumbled under his breath, "Idiot square head."

"What did you say?" Sven asked.

Annoyed that he had to be there, Jimmy said louder, "I said idiot square head. Now did you hear me?"

Sven walked up to Jimmy and snapped, "If you're going to stand on my claim, you're going to respect me."

Jimmy sized him up and decided now wasn't the time. A broad smile broke his rugged and bearded face as he spit out a chuckle. "Sven, you're doing it all wrong. I mean, can you do it that way? Yes, but you're wasting time. With each scoop, the fast-moving water is washing away a lot of your work. Don't work hard, work smart."

"Then show me," Sven said, holding the shovel out in front of him.

A loud crack in the trees above startled them.

Jimmy spun around and spotted a small face for just a second before it disappeared behind a pine tree. "There's someone spying on us."

Sven knew exactly who it was. "Oh, pay no mind. That's Jeremiah."

"Who's that?"

"A wildling boy, lives out here in the brush. He's mulatto, abandoned, I hear. I give him food now and then. He's harmless," Sven explained.

Jimmy kept his eyes glued on the tree, waiting for Jeremiah to make a reappearance, but he didn't.

"Where do we begin? You're the expert?" Sven asked, badly wanting to change the topic back to prospecting.

Jimmy looked around. The area all around Sven's claim was flat save for a rock and dirt outcropping that rose twenty-some feet above the creek. "There, have you looked over there?" he asked, pointing to the exposed side of the outcropping that faced the creek.

"No."

Jimmy tapped his finger against his temple and said, "Work smart, not hard." He strode over and began to look around while Sven just stood watching. He bent down, reached into the chest pocket of his shirt and removed a nugget of gold. "Look here!" he hollered.

Sven cocked his head and asked, "What?"

Jimmy stood up and turned around. In his fingers he held a gold nugget the size of a quarter. "Gold! I found it lying right next to a rock!"

"Huh?" Sven said and rushed over. He snatched the nugget from Jimmy's hand and examined it closely. "Impossible."

Jimmy took it back and said, "It's gold, Goddamn it. Open your eyes."

Once more, Sven grabbed the nugget. He swiftly turned around and looked at it more closely. It had the right color and appearance, but there was another way he'd heard about. He put it between his teeth and bit; he could feel the softness of the nugget. His eyes widened with joy. "I think you're right. It's gold!"

"Then we look here today. Get that shovel and start digging," Jimmy said.

Sven pocketed the gold and ran to get his shovel and bucket. "Oh my, wait 'til Anna hears."

Watching Sven react with pure glee, a crooked smile creased across Jimmy's face. He was disobeying Liam, but he had a good reason, and soon he'd let him in on it.

DEADWOOD, DAKOTA TERRITORY

John decided it was best he ride ahead to find the doctor and prepare him for Horatio's arrival. After asking several people, he was given the directions to Doc Hardy's house. Riding to the house, he was in awe at the filled streets and sheer activity of the town. He'd thought Dodge City was alive, but Deadwood was awash in overzealous excitement. He could feel the energy pouring out of everyone. Where a building didn't stand along Main Street, a tent was erected, and outside each, men peddled their wares. From chamber pots, knee-high boots, and every imaginable tool needed for mining, they were out calling out to all who would hear with hopes they'd find a buyer. But it just wasn't the proprietors of equipment; tents and tables alike sold everything any man could imagine. Whiskey by the shot, fresh venison, baths, peep shows, gold exchanges, lumber, livestock—you name it, and John swore he saw it for sale. Never in his life had he seen a place like this. He'd pass one person hollering at him to take a look at blankets; then he'd pass another shouting with hopes he'd stop and get a haircut and shave. It was a shock to the system to see such a thriving town, but he was there not to be distracted but to locate the doctor. He refocused and hurried towards his destination.

John followed the directions and soon arrived at the doctor's house. It was on the northeast side of town. The small single-level detached wood structure sat between two white canvas tents, but unlike the tents he'd seen in the heart of the town, no one was out peddling items.

He dismounted Molly, tied her up to a hitching post, and walked to the door. He'd raised his hand to knock when the front door swung open.

"Who's hurt?" an elderly man asked, pushing his eyeglasses up on his nose. He gave John a look over and again asked, "Are you deaf? Who's hurt?"

"Oh, um, a man. I believe he's got the pox," John replied.

The doctor looked past John, then turned his head to the left and right and said, "Well, where is he?"

"He's on his way to town; should arrive in a couple of hours. I rode ahead to find you so that you'll be ready to receive him when he gets here."

"You did, did ya? Hmm, let's see," the doctor said, pushing past John and going left towards one of the tents. He tossed the flap open and disappeared inside.

John followed. Inside he found rows of empty cots except for one at the far end.

"When he gets here, we'll set him up in here," the

doctor said.

"Here?" John asked, not expecting this would be the place Horatio would be treated.

"Yep, here. This is where we treated the outbreak over the summer, and it's where we care for anyone who comes to me with the pox. You see, it's important we quarantine them. After what happened over the summer, we can't risk another major outbreak."

"I don't suspect the man coming will want to stay in these conditions. He has means. Is there somewhere else he can be treated?" John said.

The doctor scowled and said, "I don't care if he's the president of the United States or the king of England. If you have the pox in Deadwood, you come here, no exceptions."

John didn't want to argue. He nodded and said, "I'll head out to meet them and bring them directly. Thank you." He tipped his hat and headed to exit the tent.

"Say, what's your name?" the doctor asked.

"John Nichols, and the man who you'll be treating is Horatio Rothman."

"Well, I'm Doc Hardy, but you can just call me Hardy or Doc even."

"Sounds good."

"Say, how will you be paying?" Hardy asked.

"Cash, we'll be paying in cash."

"Good 'cause I don't take promissory notes, only cash or gold. Hell, I've even been known to take deeds or claims, but no damn promissory notes, you hear me?"

Not looking back, John simply replied, "I hear ya."

***

Jimmy fell to the floor hard. The slap from Liam was unexpected and unnecessary. Liam had many issues, but two identifiable ones were his temper and his inability to listen long enough before making a judgment.

"I said take care of him. Does keeping that square head alive translate to taking care of him?" Liam hollered. He towered over Jimmy, who lay sprawled on Liam's office floor.

"Liam, let me finish," Jimmy urged, rubbing his cheek.

"Idiots, all of you. If I could pick you up, I'd toss you from the ruff!" Liam roared, his Midwestern accent showing through. Liam never talked about where he came from, but when he drank too much or got angry, he'd slip and say ruff when he was pronouncing roof, or crek when he meant to say creek. Liam liked people to think he was born into wealth and came from a prominent family in the east. He felt it gave him even greater stature in the town, but the truth was he was born and raised in Iowa.

"Liam, just let me finish what I was going to say," Jimmy again requested. He sat up and wiped a trickle of blood from his split lip.

Liam walked behind his desk, removed a cork from a bottle of whiskey, and poured the contents into a glass. He took the glass and drank it down with one large gulp. He poured another glass, this time emptying the bottle. Angry, he threw the bottle against the far wall. It smashed into a thousand pieces and shards. "Oliver!" he yelped.

Growing impatient, he hollered again, "Oliver!"

The door swung open, and a young man, about seventeen, rushed in, "Yes, Liam."

"Get me another bottle of whiskey," he ordered.

Oliver raced out of the room, closing the door behind him.

"And make sure it's the good stuff!" Liam hollered.

Jimmy, in the meantime, had gotten back to his feet and stood feet from Liam's desk.

"Go ahead. Finish your story," Liam said, taking a seat and putting up his feet.

"Thank you. Well, you see, I got thinking, and I figured we might be getting this claim back after Sven's accident, so I thought we'd get Sven talking about how well it's producing. That way, when we go to sell it again, we can get even more cash for it."

"I don't understand. The claim is played out. Abraham sucked what little gold there was there out of it; hence why he worked that scam with us to sell it to the first chump that walked into the bar," Liam replied.

"You see, Liam, I think Abraham talked a bit, and some people know that claim is played out, but what if we make Sven believe there's gold there by planting it? We get him to start talking about it, 'cause that's what he does best. Anyone who knows him knows he's a big talker."

"So your brilliant plan is to plant gold around for him to find, then get him to come into camp and tell everyone who will hear about how much he's pulling out of it. Then you'll take care of him. We buy the claim from the bereaved widow and sell it for a hefty profit to the next clueless miner that strolls in?"

Nodding his head with excitement, Jimmy said, "Yep, that's it."

"Hmm, you know, I like it, but let's not waste too much time. Plant more gold, get him talking, then see him off to Valhalla," Liam said.

The door burst open, and Oliver came in. He placed a dark brown bottle on the table and asked, "Will that be it, Liam?"

Liam took the bottle, pulled the cork, and poured another full glass. He took a drink then immediately spit it out. "What the hell! I said give me the good stuff. Doesn't anyone listen? Is everyone that works for me a Goddamn idiot?" Liam barked.

Young Oliver cowered at Liam's harsh words. "Sorry, Liam."

"Sorry? Take this shit away and serve it to the paying customers, and go get me a bottle of the good stuff," Liam ordered, putting the cork back in the bottle and tossing it at Oliver.

Almost fumbling the bottle, Oliver left as quickly as he could. If he stayed a second longer and suffered further abuse, he just might cry.

"Where do you hire these people?" Liam asked Jimmy.

"He's Taylor's boy. He's a good kid," Jimmy said, referring to Cartwright Taylor, one of the main bouncers who worked the room and protected the bar.

"He might be good, but he's an idiot," Liam said, shaking his head. "Anyway, I like this plan. Keep me informed."

"I'll be needing some more gold nuggets, you know, to plant for Sven," Jimmy said sheepishly.

Liam swung around in his chair and turned the combination on the safe until he unlocked it. He reached in and pulled out a metal tray. He picked up several smaller nuggets and handed them to Jimmy. "Make sure he cashes them back here."

"Yes, sir," Jimmy said.

"Oh, and what happened to Abraham?" Liam asked.

"Fed him to Avery Brown's pigs before I left this morning," Jimmy answered.

"Good, now get the hell out of my office, and on your way through the bar, send that new girl back," Liam ordered.

"Evelyn from Ohio?" Jimmy asked.

"Yeah, that one," Liam said, relaxing back into his chair.

***

The orange flame from the oil lamp reflected off the nugget in Sven's hand. He'd been staring at it for over an hour, not saying a word to Anna.

Anna didn't mind when Sven didn't talk. On the contrary, he talked so much that when he didn't, she found solace in the quiet.

"It's beautiful," Sven said, his eyes glued on the nugget.

"Yes, it is. Now can you please try on those trousers

I mended?" Anna asked.

"I will. I'm just admiring this here gold. It's perfect, just as God intended. Did you know this nugget has been around since the dawn of time, all the way back to Adam and Eve and the creation," Sven said, his eyes locked on the nugget.

"I need you to go to the mercantile and get some salt and bread, and also get some butter," Anna said, her fingers busy darning a sock.

"Why didn't you go earlier?" he asked, annoyed, finally pulling his gaze from the nugget to sneer at her.

"Because I was cleaning clothes and getting those trousers hemmed," she replied.

He pocketed the nugget and grabbed his soiled brown hat and exited the tent. The sun had set over the mountaintops, but it hadn't dipped below the horizon. He still had another half an hour of daylight left. Happy at the success at his claim, he walked with a pep in his step. With his mind on future finds, he didn't hear Jimmy shout at him.

"Sven, hey, Sven!" Jimmy hollered from the entrance of the Cricket.

Sven kept strolling, his mind filled with dreams of wealth and prosperity.

Wanting to get Sven's attention, Jimmy ran up and loudly called, "Sven, what are you doing?"

Sven looked up, a bit startled, and replied, "Heading to the merc."

"How about a drink?" Jimmy asked.

"I can't. I need to pick something up for my Anna,"

Sven replied.

"Just a drink, on me. I think you deserve to celebrate today. I promise it won't take long," Jimmy said.

Sven thought about it. He knew Anna needed the salt for preparing dinner, but the sound of a free drink was enticing. "Just one drink; then I must be on my way."

"That's the spirit. C'mon inside," Jimmy said, taking Sven by the arm and escorting him inside the Cricket.

***

Whether Sven intended it or not, his one-drink limit turned to seven, and the more he drank, the more he talked. Each time he set his glass down, Jimmy or Liam poured him another, and when they weren't pouring, they were egging him on to loudly talk about the two-ounce nugget taken from his claim, something Sven was easily obliged to do.

"Would you look at that beauty?" Sven said, slurring his words to a stranger next to him. "It's a real beauty, isn't it?"

The man nodded and went about his business.

Another man pushed his way up to Sven, snatched the nugget from his grip, and closely looked at it.

"Give that back," Sven said.

The man looked up and asked, "You found this on Saul's old claim?"

"Yes," Sven replied.

Liam nudged Jimmy, who promptly walked back from behind the bar and stood next to both Sven and the man.

"Weeks back Saul told me that claim was plum—"

And before the man could finish his comment, Jimmy took him by the arm and escorted him out, ensuring he took the nugget back before tossing him onto the street. "Don't you come back in here!" He went back up to Sven and said, "Here's your gold back.

"What do you think he was about to say?" Sven asked.

"Oh, that Saul was a fool for selling the claim," Liam blurted out.

Sven swayed a bit and continued, "Why did you remove him?"

"He's a known troublemaker, and the last thing we want for you, my dear friend, is for someone to interrupt so rudely your celebration," Liam said.

"Thank you, Liam," Sven said, nodding happily.

"Here you go, Sven," Liam said, pouring another shot. He gave Sven a close look and continued, "Would you want to get that nugget sold? We have good prices here at the Cricket, good fair exchange rates." Liam pointed to a chalkboard behind him that hung over part of the bar.

Sven squinted and read the list. "Those prices seem fair. Sure, let's do it." He handed the nugget to Liam, who promptly asked, "Cash or bar credit? I give a higher percentage for bar credit, that includes pussy too."

"No, thank you, I'll take the cash," Sven said.

"Sounds good," Liam said. He reached down and brought up a metal box from underneath and placed it on the bar. He unlocked it, removed a small scale, weighed the nugget, and proclaimed, "Two point three ounces."

Sven nodded in approval.

Liam removed a wad of cash and peeled off several bills and handed them to him. "There you go, my Northman friend."

"Thank you," Sven said, pocketing the cash.

"Sven Jacobsen!" Anna hollered from the entrance of the bar.

Everyone in the Cricket grew silent, and all eyes were on her.

She navigated through the drunken crowd and up to Sven. "I've been waiting for you."

"I decided to come celebrate my find," Sven said.

"Were you planning on coming back?" she asked, her tone telling all she was angry and annoyed.

"Woman, leave before I make you leave," Sven warned, standing tall in an attempt to intimidate her.

Laughter broke out around the bar at the spectacle of a man being chastised by his wife. Even Liam was enjoying the drama. However, for Jimmy, he found himself aroused and attracted to her. He'd seen her before but not like this—her blond hair hanging low and resting on her shoulders, her blue eyes wide and enticing, and her large chest heaving with each breath she took. He wanted her, badly.

"I'll come back when I damn well please! Now leave or I'll kick you in the arse!" Sven bellowed.

Anna looked around at the drunken and smiling faces all facing her to see what she would do or say next.

She knew her behavior was emasculating, but her anger was too much to contain. He'd lied to her, and that was unforgivable. She didn't like Deadwood for many reasons, and one was she found it to be a Godless place. And now it was dragging her beloved into its clutches.

"Leave!" Sven barked and pointed to the door.

She clenched her hands into fists as the temptation to strike him washed over her, but she relented and turned to go.

Chuckles and laughter rose in volume as she exited the bar. The last thing she heard as she stepped off the walkway was Sven proudly telling the bar that he'd shown her.

With Anna gone, Sven returned to drinking and bragging.

***

John reached the others just an hour outside town to find Horatio's condition had gotten slightly worse. His fever was worse, and the rash had spread. He could tell by the look on William's face that he was concerned.

"I found a doctor. He's expecting us," John said to William.

"Good and thank you," William said.

Trotting next to William, John continued, "I should tell you that he'll be quarantined in a tent next to the doctor's residence."

"Tent?" William asked, shocked to hear about the accommodations.

"Apparently the so-called lawless town has rules, and one of them is anyone with pox must be quarantined there, period," John explained.

"It will be fine. I'm just worried. Did you happen to see a telegraph office? I want to send a message back to Mother in New York," William said.

"I didn't see one, but I'm sure you'll find one," John said.

The last hour into town was slow as the traffic heading in grew in size.

When they reached the outskirts of Deadwood, William marveled at the excitement much like John had.

"We're close. It's just at the far end of town," John said.

Commotion broke out to their right as two men spilled out into the middle of the street, their fists flying. Both were miners, but that was where any likeness or similarity ended. One man was tall and large while the other was short and lean.

John slowed Molly and looked for a way around, but a crowd was growing to watch the men fight. Unable to get around, John came to a full stop. He watched as the men bloodied themselves.

A look of excitement washed over William. He'd never really watched a grown man fight like that; it was very much a new experience outside of watching John gun down people. He leaned in to John and said, "My money is on the big guy."

John watched the two men wrestle and came to the conclusion that the smaller man would prevail barring the large man striking him perfectly. What he saw in the smaller man was a bigger heart and that he knew how to throw a good punch. "I'll take that bet. Twenty dollars the smaller man wins."

William stretched out his hand and said, "Let's shake."

They shook and went back to watching the brawl.

Just as John predicted, the smaller man had better moves and threw accurate punches. As the large man came at the young man, he simply stepped to the side, struck him with a blow to the side of the face, and kicked him in the side of the knee.

The bigger man fell to the ground but wasn't out. He reached down, pulled a knife from his boot, and held it up just as the smaller man jumped at him, resulting in him being impaled on the blade. He howled in pain and recoiled back, but the bigger man was not about to let go. He plunged the knife several more times.

The smaller man fell onto his side, coughed up a large amount of blood, and groaned in pain. "He stabbed me. The son of a bitch stabbed me."

Seeing his opportunity to finish the fight once and for all, the bigger man rolled onto the smaller man, held the knife high, and plunged it into his chest.

The younger man gasped once and died, his eyes left open.

The bigger man removed the bloody blade, wiped it on his trousers, and reinserted the knife into the sheath in his boot.

"Looks like you owe me twenty dollars, Mr.

Nichols," William said with a cocky tone.

"Take it out of my pay," John sneered.

They rode by the grisly scene and continued towards Doc Hardy's house.

"Wasn't that exciting?" William asked. The brief interlude had given him a small amount of respite from his ill father.

"I suppose," John said.

"And no one will go to jail? Two men fight, one kills the other, and that's it?" William asked.

"Well, murder isn't condoned. The man who murdered Will Bill was tried—"

"Yes, but he was acquitted," William said, interrupting John.

"Correct, but it was tried. That back there was a fight and by most standards will be considered a justified death," John said.

"Fascinating," William said with a smile.

After riding through the bustling streets, they made it to Doc Hardy's house and were greeted promptly. "Take the sick man into that tent," Hardy ordered, his shirt covered in blood.

John gave him a look and asked, "You working?"

"When am I not around here? Men coming in with all sorts of wounds, many accidents but many not. This damn town never sleeps, nor can I. I can't remember the last time I had a full night's sleep," Hardy replied.

"If you don't like it, why do you stay?" John asked.

Hardy raised his right brow and declared, "Who said I didn't like it?"

William and Hans carried Horatio into the tent and placed him on the first cot they saw. Hardy came in right behind them. "Clear out of the way," Hardy said. He lowered the blanket that covered Horatio and unbuttoned his shirt to find the rash was now spread across his chest and belly. "It's smallpox alright. How long as he been sick?"

"Since yesterday," William answered.

Hardy furrowed his brow and shoved his glasses up on his nose and said, "Impossible. His blisters are more advanced. I'd say he's been sick for four to five days."

"Sir, I can tell you that's not true. He complained last night about being extremely tired then woke up like this," William challenged.

"Son, I've been doing this a long time. This man has been sick for more than a day," Hardy said.

"He's right," Horatio mumbled.

All eyes turned to Horatio.

Hardy asked, "When did you first notice you didn't feel well?"

"Four days back, I had aches and a fever. I felt fatigued, but I didn't want to stop. I thought it was the trip. Never imagined I had smallpox," Horatio admitted.

William stepped forward, "Father, why not tell me?"

"I didn't want you to worry," Horatio answered, his eyes glassy and dried lips cracked.

"Doc, could he have infected us?" John asked.

"Why, of course. Did anyone drink after him?" Hardy asked.

Everyone shook their head.

"Have you come into contact with any of his bodily fluids?" Hardy asked, looking at each man.

Hans vigorously shook his head and grunted, "Damn fool."

"Don't you dare talk about my father that way," William snapped, his spine growing erect.

"William, it's fine," Horatio said, his voice sounding weak.

"But, Father—" William said but was stopped short.

"No, it's fine," Horatio replied, using all the strength he had to raise his hand and motion for him to be quiet.

William, disciplined from youth, did as his father commanded.

"Go, all of you. This man is sick and needs to rest. He can't do that with you hovering around," Hardy said, ushering everyone towards the exit.

"Wait, John, come," Horatio beckoned.

John gave everyone a look and settled on Hardy. "He's asking?"

"Sure, but make it quick," Hardy replied.

All but John left the tent, leaving him with Horatio and one other sick individual at the far end. John made his way to within a few feet and stopped. "What can I do for you?"

"Sorry I wasn't honest," Horatio said and coughed.

"You okay?" John asked.

"No, I'm not, but don't worry. I brought you here for a reason. My son, William, he needs someone like you more than ever. This town, this place, it will swallow him whole. Promise me you'll honor our arrangement and watch over him."

Not needing a second to think, John quickly replied, "Of course. I gave you my word."

"Good man, thank you. He's still a boy, really, a boy in a man's body. I blame my wife for that. He's been coddled his entire life. When he came up with this idea to mine gold, I was hesitant, but soon saw it could be the perfect place to shape him into the man I need him to be."

John nodded slightly, understanding the wants and desires of a parent are powerful motivators.

"You see, William will take over my company when I die, and I need a man to run that, not a spoiled boy. Watch over him. It's okay if he gets a few bruises and scrapes, just guide him through."

"Yes, sir."

"I knew we chose right. Thank you."

"You bet."

"Now leave. I need to rest. You can send the doctor in. I have a few questions to ask him. And make sure William pays you what we owe."

John nodded and said, "I will. You get some rest."

Horatio closed his eyes and sighed.

John exited to find Hardy and William talking while Hans was standing next to the wagon, doing what he normally did, smoke. "Hey, Doc, he wants to see you."

"Sure thing, and come back tomorrow if you want. I told your friend if anything drastically changes, I'll send word."

"How will you find us?" John asked.

"Because I told your friend where to stay. It's the best place in town," Hardy said, disappearing into the tent.

"What did my father want?" William asked.

Lying, John answered, "Told me to proceed with getting the claim up and running and not to worry about him."

"First thing we should do is find a place to stay and a good livery for the horses," Hans said, overhearing their conversation.

"Hans is right. Let's settle in then go check out the claim," John said.

All agreed and left for the hotel.

CHAPTER THREE

"If you tell the truth, you don't have to remember anything." – Mark Twain

DEADWOOD, DAKOTA TERRITORY

SEPTEMBER 26, 1876

Sven set out early, leaving Anna lying in bed. He had arrived home hours after she'd encountered him at the bar, drunk and belligerent. She questioned why she had even attempted to retrieve him. As she lay staring at the off-white canvas ceiling, she wondered how long she'd have to endure life in Deadwood. Even though he'd spent their life savings on the claim, she found solace in knowing that if he failed, they'd soon be heading back to Minnesota. But now with the prospects looking up, their departure seemed to be growing remote.

A shadow cast over the tent, and she called out, "Did you forget something?"

The tent flap opened, bringing with it the dawn's early light and blinding her to who was now standing in the entrance.

She sat up, shielded her eyes and asked, "Sven, is that you?"

"It's me, Jimmy."

Fear gripped her. She covered herself and pulled herself into a ball as far away from him as possible. "Sven isn't here. He went to the claim."

"I know where he is," Jimmy said, taking a couple of steps towards her. "I'm meeting him there shortly."

"What do you want?" Her voice cracked.

"After seeing you last night, I had no idea you were so beautiful. I just wanted to stop by and tell you," he replied, taking another step closer.

"Leave," she yelled.

"I'm not here to hurt you. I just wanted to cast my eyes on you again. I couldn't get you out of my mind after seeing you yesterday," Jimmy said, his tone gentle but devious. "I would take better care of you. I could give you more than he can. A house, a real bed with sheets, and your very own kitchen with a stove."

"This is inappropriate. Leave or I'll scream," she snapped.

"I'm leaving, but know I think you're a real beauty," Jimmy said and hastily exited the tent as fast as he'd entered it.

She watched in terror as his shadow slipped away. Exhaling heavily, she began to cry. Never in her life had she felt so threatened, so vulnerable. It was this place, she hated it. Now more than ever she wanted to leave.

***

After breakfast the three separated. William to go visit his father, then proceed to secure the notarized paperwork for the claim, Hans to go prepare the wagon and horses for the supply run and subsequent ride to the claim, and

John to get the equipment and tools they'd need.

John went to the first hardware store he saw near the hotel. He entered and found the establishment busy but not so much that someone didn't ask if he needed assistance.

"Howdy, what can I do you for?" a short and small man asked, a white apron wrapped around him.

John removed his hat and replied, "I'm looking for an entire kit for prospecting. Make it enough so three people can work."

"You'll be needing everything?" the man asked.

"Yes, everything," John said, looking around the store. From floor to ceiling the shop was full of supplies.

"We'll get you covered, don't you worry. My name is Stephen. I'm one of the owners of this establishment. Over there is my business partner, Phillip," Stephen said, holding his hand out.

John shook his hand and replied, "Nice to meet you. My name is John."

"I hear an accent. You from the South?"

"Yeah."

"Whereabouts?" Stephen asked.

"Listen, I'm on a tight schedule. Do you mind getting what I need?" John asked, not wishing to have a conversation.

Hearing John's answer, Phillip came from behind the counter and up to John and Stephen. "Go get the man his wares."

"Thank you."

"Stephen means well. He likes to get to know the

customers is all," Phillip said.

"Not a problem, just on a schedule," John said, his eyes darting around at all the items around him.

"You're new in town?"

"You all ask a lot of questions," John said, fixing his gaze directly on Phillip. He looked down and saw he was wearing a gun belt.

"Stephen likes to get to know our customers. I like to know who our customers are," Phillip clarified.

"Phillip, I'm just here to get some supplies and equipment; then I'll be joining some others to go work a claim. That's it."

"I'll take that as a yes, being you're new to town. Stay away from Liam Prince and any of his people at the Cricket. Don't do any business with him, period."

"He's untrustworthy?" John asked.

"That's putting it lightly. Just avoid him and his place. If you be needing a drink, go to the Bella Union or the Number Ten Saloon."

"How do you know I'm not friends with this Liam Prince?" John asked.

"'Cause you look like an honest man," Phillip replied.

Stephen came up, a broad smile on his face. "I have all your stuff assembled in the back. You can pick it up there off the alley."

"Thank you," John said.

"You ready to settle up?" Stephen asked, wiping his hands on his apron.

"Sure," John said and stepped off to follow him up to the counter but stopped, turned to face Phillip and said, "Thank you for the advice. It's much appreciated."

"Anytime. We aim to please here at Barns Hardware," Phillip said, a slight grin appearing beneath his thick mustache.

John nodded and went to the counter to conclude his business with Stephen.

***

Horatio's condition hadn't improved, but it also hadn't worsened. William found that piece of information to mean things were looking up. With his visit complete, he rode to the office of Samuel Atkins, Esquire, a local attorney and the man he had secured the claim from after reading an advertisement in his local paper months before. He tied his horse to a hitching post and made his way inside.

The small office was at the most sixty square feet, enough to fit a desk and several chairs. A burly man behind the desk looked up, removed his spectacles and asked, "Good morning, sir. What can I do for you?"

"Hello, my name is William Rothman. I'm here to pick up the paperwork for my claim," William said. He fidgeted with his hat as he held it.

"Hmm, a Mr. William Rothman. The name doesn't sound familiar. When did you secure this claim?" Samuel asked.

"That would have been five months ago this week. I saw an advertisement in the *Post* and wrote. You replied saying you had a claim. I had the money wired through my bank, the New York First Bank and Trust Company. Here is the letter from you and the confirmation of the monies sent as well as a letter signed by a Samuel Atkins, Esquire, confirming receipt of funds and instructions to pick up the notarized claim upon arrival in Deadwood," William said, pulling the paperwork from his inside jacket pocket and handing it to Samuel.

Samuel put on his spectacles and read the paperwork. A bead of sweat appeared on his forehead. "Oh, yes. The Deadwood Creek fork two claim. Yes, I now remember. Let me go and pull it from my file in the back." Samuel stood and exited through a door at the back of the room.

William walked the small space, stopping when he saw a map of Deadwood.

The door opened, and Samuel stepped in with a nervous look on his face. "Ah, Mr...."

"Rothman," William said, seeing he'd forgotten his last name.

"Yes, Mr. Rothman, there appears to have been a mistake, I fear."

"What sort of mistake?" William asked.

"The claim you purchased was sold to another person two months ago," Samuel said sheepishly.

"You sold my claim?"

"Unfortunately, yes, it was a clerical error. Apparently the title was never entered, so therefore you never actually purchased the claim."

"But you took my money!" William said, exasperated.

"We did, and we'll promptly refund you the monies in full. That I promise."

"I don't want my money refunded. I want my claim, or a claim. Now go back or wherever you need to go and give me a claim," William asserted.

"Sir, I wish I could, really, but the unfortunate thing is…there aren't any claims to be had," Samuel said reluctantly.

"No claims to be had? I purchased mine nearly five months ago. I have a letter there confirming it, you took my money, you gave me a confirmation letter. Now, where is my claim?"

"All that is correct, sir, but the problem is that it was never entered in by the camp clerk. Title was never drafted, sir, meaning there is no claim with your name on it. I so apologize for this error, and I can assure you, we'll refund your money right away," Samuel said.

Anger swelled in William; he wasn't used to being told no. He took a step towards Samuel and barked, "Give me a claim!"

"Sir, what I can do is suggest you talk to miners in town, see if they'll sell you theirs, or go visit the proprietors of the local establishments. They always hear about available claims. Oh, you should go see Mr. Prince at the Cricket. He always seems to know someone selling a claim."

William's anger moderated after Samuel gave him options. "A Mr. Prince at the Cricket?"

"Yes, sir, it's several doors down. Go see him and tell him I sent you down."

"When will I get my money back?" William asked.

"Come back in a couple of hours. I'll have it then," Samuel said.

William snatched the paperwork from Samuel's grip and marched out the door. He looked left and saw a sign that read *CRICKET—BEER, WHISKEY & FINE ENTERTAINMENT*. He stepped off the walkway and headed towards a rendezvous with Liam Prince.

***

The second Jimmy had returned from Sven's claim, he was told Liam needed to see him. Not wasting a second, he rushed to Liam's office to find him covering the rules for some new ladies he had just employed.

Seeing Jimmy standing there, he ended his briefing and sent the girls away. "Get in here and close the door," he ordered.

Jimmy did what was asked and went to go sit. His feet and legs were weary from a full day of work.

"No sitting down, no time. I need you to head right back out and get that square head," Liam said.

"What for?" Jimmy asked.

"Plan has changed."

"You want me to kill him?" Jimmy asked.

"No, we're not going to kill him. We're going to convince him to sell us the claim; then we're going to turn around and sell it to this wealthy asshole who rolled into town yesterday. You should see the guy. He has money falling out of every orifice," Liam said, laughing.

"But Sven won't sell, especially after today. He found two nuggets I planted. The guy thinks he's gonna be rich," Jimmy said.

Liam leaned over his desk and said, "Then we'll have to do a good job convincing him. Go get that square head and bring him back here, now."

"Liam, this ain't gonna work," Jimmy said.

"Let me do the thinking. Your plan was good, but this is better," Liam said.

"Why don't you just have me take them both out, and we'll just take the claim for ourselves. That was the original plan, wasn't it?" Jimmy asked.

"No, the original plan had you killing the square head. I'd then convince the wife to sell me the claim. Why did you think I was going to have her killed? Good God, man, I don't kill women…unless they have it coming, but I don't kill innocent women or children. Now get your ass out of here and bring Sven back here," Liam barked.

Disgruntled, Jimmy left.

Liam kicked his feet up on the desk and began to hum a tune.

***

The second John heard the name Liam Prince, he recoiled at first then laughed. The three had met up, with John and Hans thinking they were going out to the claim only to be told there wasn't a claim to go to. With nowhere to be, they found themselves standing at the Number Ten Saloon, having whiskey.

"What's funny?" William asked.

"The man at the hardware store warned me about that man. Told me very specifically not to do any business with him. The irony of it is funny," John explained.

"What are we going to do?" Hans asked.

"I'm going to buy a claim from this Liam Prince no matter what you say. I came all this way to prospect and mine, and damn it, that's what I'm going to do," William said defiantly. He picked up a shot full of whiskey and tossed it back.

"That man from the hardware store was adamant about not doing business with Prince. Maybe you should talk to the man at the hardware store," John said.

"I'm not going to get my professional advice from a clerk," William mocked. "Barkeep, another whiskey."

"There's nothing I can say to convince you?" John asked.

"I studied business at Columbia University. I know what I'm doing," William said proudly, holding his head high.

John rolled his eyes and shook his head.

Seeing John's response, William snarked, "Did you even attend university?"

"No," John answered.

"Mr. Nichols…John, I trust you to protect me. You're good at that; it's your expertise. Business is mine. Let's keep to what we know, okay?"

"Whatever you say," John said. A thought popped in his head that soon everything was going to go sideways.

"I'll be right back. Need to go take a piss," William

said and walked out the back of the saloon.

Hans patted John on the shoulder and said, "I'm going back to the hotel. I'm tired, and all of this talk of buying claims is boring. I'll see you in the morning." Hans tossed back his final shot and left.

All John could do was think of how he could find a way to convince William his plan was a bad idea.

"Barns is right," a man said farther down the bar.

John glanced over at the man and asked, "What do you know?"

The bartender quipped, "Watch yourself. He's a Pinkerton man."

His curiosity piqued, John asked, "What's a Pinkerton doing in Deadwood?"

The man walked around and took a spot next to John. He extended his hand and said, "Garrett Vane. Pleasure to meet you."

"John Nichols," John said, shaking Garrett's hand.

"I couldn't help but overhear your conversation with your compatriot. I hope you'll forgive me," Garrett said.

"You didn't answer my question. What's a Pinkerton doing in Deadwood?"

"What do you think a Pinkerton is doing here?" Garrett replied.

"Let me ask again, who are you investigating?" John asked.

"A missing person. I was sent weeks ago. My client is a United States senator. His son came to Deadwood in July and has since disappeared."

"Being that you're still here tells me you haven't

solved the case," John said, pouring himself another drink. He held up the bottle and said, "You want a pour?"

"Sure."

John filled Garrett's glass and asked, "Any leads?"

"I have a suspect but not a shred of evidence to do anything with."

"Let me guess, your suspect is Liam Prince," John quipped.

"Everyone is a suspect at first," he joked. "But no, it appears this might have been all about a poker game gone bad. However, as it pertains to Prince, all I've heard is that man is as crooked as they come."

"Maybe you can help me convince my colleague that doing business with him is not a sound idea," John said.

William showed up suddenly and asked, "What's not a sound idea?"

Garrett turned and stuck out his hand. "Garrett Vane, Pinkerton Detective Agency."

Excited, William shook his hand and said, "A real-life Pinkerton. Tell me, what thrilling case are you working on?"

"Missing person."

"Anyone I would know?" William asked.

"A son of a United States senator, his name is Maxwell Harrison," Garrett answered.

William thought for a second and said, "Never heard of him." He nudged John and said, "Time to go."

"Garrett agrees that you shouldn't do business with Mr. Prince. He's heard the same thing—the man is not to be trusted," John said, hoping Garrett's reputation as a

Pinkerton would sway him.

"Must I repeat myself? I'm the businessman, you're the security, and this Pinkerton is an investigator. Let's all stay in our places," William said.

Garrett smiled and said, "With that, I'll say my goodbyes." Garrett headed back to his place at the bar.

"Now come, John, I don't want to be late," William said.

***

When Sven returned to the tent, excited by his find, Anna decided then not to tell him about Jimmy. Though she was upset with him, she loved him dearly, and taking away from his joy didn't feel right.

"Look at them, Anna. Aren't they beautiful?" Sven asked, extending his arm with his open hand facing up. Inside were the two nuggets. One was the size of the one the day before, but the second was larger.

"They're beautiful," she said, stirring a pot over the fire.

Sven looked up towards the late afternoon sky and said, "Dear Lord, thank you. Thank you for this gift. You have blessed me and my wife."

A tear came to Anna's eye. It had been a long time since she'd seen Sven pray. He hadn't been the most religious man, and that was fine, but for him to break out in spontaneous prayer was very uncommon.

"Sven, get your boots on," Jimmy hollered from a distance.

Anna and Sven looked back and saw Jimmy heading their way.

Nervous and unable to look at him, Anna got up and headed into the tent.

Sven waved and said, "Jimmy, not tonight. I can't go to the bar, sorry."

Jimmy stopped and said, "It's not about drinking, it's business. Liam needs to speak with you. It's very important."

"Oh, what is it?" Sven asked.

"Call it an opportunity. Now, c'mon, put your boots on."

A flood of feelings washed over Sven. *What does Liam want?* he thought. *Opportunity? Am I about to be offered something unimaginable from a man of Liam's stature?* Excited to find out, he put on his boots and hollered to Anna, "I'll be right back. Liam wants to see me. It's an opportunity."

Anna hid but didn't say a word.

Not waiting for her reply, Sven got up and started for the Cricket.

Jimmy patiently stood there with hopes Anna would poke her head out, but she didn't. Not wanting Sven to get too far ahead, he chased after him.

***

Sven was as giddy as a child on Christmas when he entered the Cricket. Thoughts of opulence and influence kept popping into his mind. He began to imagine Liam offering him a piece of the Cricket itself. As he waded through the sea of drunk men and scantily dressed women, his big toothy smile was ever present.

Jimmy knocked on Liam's door. "It's Jimmy. I have Sven here."

"Come in, come in," Liam said, standing up.

Sven and Jimmy walked in.

Liam walked over and greeted Sven. "My good man, it is good to see you."

Sven shook his hand and replied, "It's good to see you too."

"Take a seat, please. Can I get you a drink, a whiskey maybe? How about some of my good stuff, my personal stash?" Liam offered.

Sven sat and looked around. Thoughts of this being his office soon came to him.

Liam poured a big glass of whiskey and placed it in front of Sven. "Here you go, my friend."

"Thank you, Liam, but I shouldn't drink," Sven said.

"Oh c'mon. Is this because of last night?" Liam asked.

"I promised my Anna I'd hurry back," Sven replied.

"I'm not asking you to get drunk, I'm merely offering you a drink," Liam explained.

Sven thought for a second, nodded and grabbed the glass. He gave Liam a smile and took a big gulp. "The good stuff," he said with a smile.

"That it is," Liam said.

"What is this opportunity you want to speak to me about?" Sven asked.

Liam gave Jimmy a look and answered the question with a question, "What did Jimmy tell you?"

"Nothing, just that you had an opportunity for me."

"That I do. A big opportunity and an apology," Liam confided.

Sven was drinking when Liam used the word *apology*. He coughed and put his glass down. "For what?"

"First let me tell you the opportunity."

Sven nodded.

"We want to buy your claim back for ten percent more than you bought it for," Liam said plainly.

Sven gave Liam and Jimmy both an odd look before he replied, "Buy it back. Is this a joke?"

"No, we want to buy it from you."

Seeing Liam's serious look, Sven said, "You mean it."

"I do."

"It's not for sale. I would never sell that claim; it's just producing. No, I won't sell for ten percent more or a hundred percent more. I won't do it. That claim is going to make me a rich man, richer than you, Liam Prince."

Liam laughed and said, "Now onto that apology. That claim we sold you, it is played out. We sold you a bogus claim. Saul was in here complaining about his claim not producing, so we came up with a way to scam someone, and it happened that you were the one who got scammed. But to make up for that lie, we want to buy it back for ten percent more than we sold it to you for."

"You're lying," Sven snapped.

"I lied then; I'm not lying now," Liam replied.

"I'm finding gold on there now, big nuggets, two-plus ounces. I found at least five ounces today. There's gold there, and you want it all for yourself. I won't sell it, you hear me?" Sven said, standing up, his nostrils flared and face red with anger.

"Sit back down. We're not done talking," Liam said.

"No, to hell with you, Liam. You bring me in here so you can lie and scam me out of my claim because I'm making money on it. Well, I won't be scammed. I won't be lied to even by a man like you!"

Liam stood and walked around the side of the desk. He was now several feet from Sven, who stood with an aggressive posture. "We were talking nicely, but you had to ruin it by getting angry. Now you're cursing and telling me, the owner of this place, to go to hell. This is my home. You don't tell me to go to hell, do you understand me?"

"Ah, screw you! My claim is producing, and soon enough I'll have more money than you. I'll come back and buy this place," Sven charged.

"You shut your mouth, you insolent bastard," Liam warned.

Jimmy took a few steps towards them and readied for a fight.

"I'm not selling my claim, and as of this moment, Jimmy is no longer needed. How dare you bring me in here just so you can lie and cheat me out of my claim. I'm going to make you more famous than you are, I'm gonna let the entire camp know you're a lying and cheating son of a whore."

Liam lunged at him and grabbed Sven by the throat.

Sven easily broke his grasp and shoved Liam hard across the room.

Liam looked at Jimmy and nodded.

Taking his cue, Jimmy pulled a Colt from his side holster, cocked, aimed and pulled the trigger. The bullet slammed into the back of Sven's head and exited his face on the right side of his nose.

Sven didn't make a sound. He dropped where he stood and was dead before he hit the ground.

Liam walked over and spat on him. "To hell with you, you square head bastard."

Jimmy holstered the Colt and asked, "Now what do we do?"

"Plan C," Liam said.

"What's that?" Jimmy asked.

"Do I have to spell it out for you?" Liam sneered, stepping over a pool of blood that was gathering. He walked up to Jimmy and got inches from his face. "Dispose of him, clean up this mess, and go take care of the wife."

"You mean?" Jimmy asked.

"You know what I mean."

***

William stopped before he and John entered the Cricket. "Let me do all the talking. Remember, this is my world." He turned and sauntered into the rowdy bar.

John followed William inside without saying a word.

William went to the bar and called out, "Barkeep, I

need two whiskeys, and I need to see Mr. Prince."

The bartender placed two shot glasses down and filled them. "I'll go get Liam."

William took his glass and said, "Raise your glass, as we're about to have ourselves a claim."

John kept his mouth shut and tapped William's glass reluctantly.

Liam arrived and took up a spot behind the bar. "Good day, gentlemen, how are we?"

"Liam, this is John Nichols. He works for me."

"Mr. Nichols," Liam said, nodding.

Jumping right into business, William asked, "Liam, do you have that claim to sell?"

"As a matter of fact, my man James here does. I'm helping to broker the deal, nothing more. He'll just need to get the paperwork handled tomorrow, but you're more than free to go work the claim in the morning, and upon your return, he can make it official," Liam said.

"Excellent. How much was it again?" William asked.

"Twenty-two thousand dollars," Liam said confidently without blinking an eye.

"All I have is twenty, will you take it?" William countered.

"Twenty on you now?" Liam asked.

William pulled a wad of cash from his pocket and slapped it on the bar. "Twenty thousand. Take it or leave it."

Liam went to reach for the money, but John put his hand on top of his. "Maybe we should inspect this claim first. How do we know this is a good claim?"

"'Cause it is," Liam answered.

"But how do we know you're not just selling some dirt that doesn't have gold on it?" John asked.

William stood frozen. He had opened his mouth, but no words came out.

"You can trust James…it's Mr. Nichols, right?" Liam asked.

"It is."

"Where are you from?" Liam asked.

"Why does everyone have to ask me that?"

"Liam, maybe John has a point. We should take a look at the claim tomorrow, and we'll get back to you afterwards," William conceded.

"Deal is off," Liam threatened.

"No, wait," William pleaded.

"He's bluffing," John said.

"I could be, but the deal is off. If you want to buy the claim, it's back at twenty-two thousand. Hell, by tomorrow if it's still available, it will be twenty-four thousand," Liam said.

A worried look swept over William's face. "Can we go see it tonight?"

"It's too dark. We need to check it out in the morning," John suggested.

"Wait a minute. I was about to secure a claim sight unseen from Mr. Atkins, how is this any different?" William asked John.

"It's different, trust me," John said.

"I agree with Mr. Rothman. The claims the good esquire used to sell all were sold sight unseen, and that's what this deal is. If you want it now, I'll sell for twenty. If it's tomorrow, the price will be twenty-four."

"We come back tomorrow," John insisted.

"Stop! Stop interfering. Remember your place," William snapped at John.

"My place is to protect you. This is my job," John said sternly.

"That look, I swear that look you give me sometimes is frightening. I'm wondering if you're mad or about ready to kill me."

"What look?" John asked.

"That one," William said, pointing at John's hardened face.

"William, this is not a good idea," John again stressed.

Unable to relinquish his pride, William turned to face Liam, held out his hand, and said, "Deal, I'll take it for twenty."

Liam called out, "Jimmy, come and shake this man's hand."

Jimmy, who had been standing by quietly, took William's hand and shook. "It's a deal." He picked up the cash and pocketed it. "Come by in the morning. I'll take you to the claim."

CHAPTER FOUR

"It's not what you look at that matters, it's what you see." – Henry David Thoreau

DEADWOOD CREEK, FIVE MILES OUTSIDE DEADWOOD, DAKOTA TERRITORY

SEPTEMBER 27, 1876

Just as agreed upon, Jimmy escorted them to the claim, showed them the boundaries, and even told them about Jeremiah just in case he showed up.

The plan was simple: do for William as they had done for Sven, leave some nuggets over the next month to be found to keep them interested and focused; then when the claim was discovered to have been played out, they couldn't say they hadn't found something.

After Jimmy departed, leaving the men to set up, William climbed the rock outcropping to get a better vantage point of his claim. With each breath he took of the cool and dry morning air, the more exhilarated he felt. Six months before he had been a lost man, searching for a purpose, in need of an adventure. When he read the advertisement in the *Post*, he'd instantly felt the romance of being a pioneer and knew he needed to be a part of something epic. He was tired of reading about others' adventures. He wanted to create his own, and now here he was, the owner of a gold mining claim, living in a lawless town where a mere handshake concluded a deal and the sophistication of his life in New York was as distant as the Moon is to the Earth. He looked down with glee as John and Hans set up the site. He had studied every manual and book on gold prospecting, so he was confident he'd prevail. Thoughts of returning to New York and seeing his childhood friends ran through his mind. He'd be the talk of the cocktail parties and dinners. He would be heralded, and the women would swoon. He'd brag that he'd drunk whiskey in the very bar where Wild Bill was killed, and had witnessed firsthand bloody fights where two men fought and one man walked away. He'd tell his gentlemen friends over a glass of brandy about the prostitutes and general mayhem of life in a place like Deadwood. Yes, he would return a hero of sorts, and today marked that pivotal moment.

"I should have ordered a camera to be brought here. You know, I'll do that tomorrow. We need to mark this occasion," William shouted down.

"A camera?" John asked.

"Oh yes, the boy likes to take photographs. Not a party he'd host back in New York was a cameraman not present," Hans said, taking hold of a large wood crate and dragging it off the wagon.

John took a breath and looked around. The sound of the creek rushing over the rocks and the rustling of the leaves on the trees gave him pause. It was a beautiful place. "The trees are beginning to change color. Autumn will be upon us soon, then winter right behind her."

"I'm already thinking about that. I'm ordering some

wood tomorrow, meeting a man in town; he has a logging operation. I'm buying enough for us to build a shack. We'll need it for those winter months to keep warm. Plus I've sketched this," Hans said, unfolding a piece of paper. On it he had drawn a slide.

"What is it?" John asked.

"A slide, I was thinking of having it over there. I think we should divert the creek from there and have it come back over there. Then we'll start digging, we'll drop it at the top of the slide and sift through it on the slide, and it will dump out at the end."

"Oh, I see," John said, understanding the concept.

William appeared and asked, "What are you two looking at?"

"My sketch for a slide," Hans replied, handing him the paper.

William nodded and said, "Looks good. I like it, I like it."

Hans shared his thoughts with William, and surprisingly, he was receptive.

William draped his arms over Hans' and John's shoulders and said, "Men, we will be successful here. Money is no object. For I feel today is the first day of our new lives."

DEADWOOD, DAKOTA TERRITORY

The second Jimmy walked into the Cricket, Liam summoned him. "James, here you are. Come, let me pour you a coffee, and do share with me the morning's news."

Jimmy slowly walked up and leaned against the bar. He noticed the place was empty save for a couple cleaning and one mopping. He gave Liam an odd look and asked, "Where is everyone?"

"It's Wednesday," Liam replied.

"I thought today was Tuesday," Jimmy said. He rested his full weight on the bar and lowered his head. The gravity of everything that had transpired over the night and morning was taking its toll on him physically and emotionally. The dark circles under his eyes and the sunken jowls told Liam his man was beyond fatigue.

"You look like shit," Liam said, pushing a steaming cup of coffee towards Jimmy.

Jimmy picked up the coffee and took a drink. His hands were shaking a little, but it was enough for Liam to notice.

"What's happened? Why are you shaking?" Liam asked, concerned. He looked around to ensure no one was in earshot.

"I'm tired is all. I haven't eaten either," Jimmy said, placing the cup down and rubbing his cold hands.

"As a reward, go take one, hell, take two girls up and have them draw you a hot bath. It's on me," Liam offered.

"I'd prefer to just go to my place and rest," Jimmy said, his eyes rarely connecting with Liam's.

"When a man turns down pussy, something is wrong. Tell me," Liam insisted.

Weary and not wanting to have this conversation, he decided to talk about William. "Appears the rich kid plans on really setting up quite the operation. His wagon was full, and I heard talk of building on the site."

"Oh yeah, well, he's wasting his time." Liam laughed.

"I'll go by in the early evening and plant some gold," Jimmy said.

"Good. And the Jacobsens—all taken care of?" Liam asked.

"Yes, Brown's pigs won't need to eat for days," Jimmy said.

"Tell me, did Mrs. Jacobsen cower and cry, or did she fight? She looked like a scrapper the other night," Liam asked.

Jimmy took a big gulp of his coffee and said, "If you don't need me, I'll be heading back to my place."

"Fine, go, get some rest," Liam said.

Jimmy turned and headed towards the door.

Liam called out to him, "Big bonus for you this month."

Not looking or responding, Jimmy merely waved and exited the bar.

***

William sat staring at the tent where his father was quarantined. He was excited to share his day, but seeing him in his present condition would also take away from one of the most thrilling days he'd ever had. He also knew his father would ask if he'd contacted his mother. He hadn't, so he'd have to lie, something he didn't like to do.

Hardy exited his office, stopped and asked, "You been sitting there for ten minutes or more. Everything alright?"

"Yes, I'm fine. How is Father?" William asked, dismounting.

"Did I tell you yet?"

"Tell me what?"

"I don't bullshit people. Yes, I know it's not considered good bedside manner, but after years of working in the field hospitals during the war, I came to know that it was best to tell someone straight up. There's no value in lying to a person. If they're gonna die, tell them; better they have time to prepare."

"Is Father dying?" William asked, his face turning white.

"Dying? No, no, he's not dying...yet. I suppose we're all dying technically. Each day brings us closer to our death."

"Doctor, is my father dying from smallpox?" William clarified, his tone showing he was annoyed by Hardy's rambling.

"Son, he's not dying, but he's also not doing well. His fever is high, he won't eat, and he started vomiting this morning."

Hating the news, William asked, "Can I see him?"

"Of course, just stay clear, no touching. He's highly contagious," Hardy said, walking over to the tent and opening the flap.

William walked in. The first thing he noticed was the man who had been in the far corner was gone. "The man who was back there. Where is he?"

"Dead, died this morning," Hardy replied bluntly.

"Was it pox?"

"No, poor son of a bitch had typhoid. He came in on a wagon train two weeks ago. He was the last of the bunch. When they arrived, all were sick. I had them all quarantined here."

William approached his father, stopping a few feet away. He stood and listened to Horatio's labored breathing for a couple of minutes before turning to go.

"William?" Horatio asked, his voice weak.

Turning back around, William answered, "Father, hello. I didn't want to wake you. I stopped by to check on you."

"Come closer," Horatio said.

"The doctor said to stay at a distance. What do you need?"

"Your mother, have you sent a telegram?" Horatio asked.

Unable to lie, he answered, "No, but right after I leave, I'll do that. I've been very busy. Today was our first day at the claim. You should see it. We have two hundred feet of creek frontage, and the surrounding area is beautiful. It's truly God's country."

"I look forward to spending time with you there," Horatio said.

"I also look forward to that. You'll be proud of me, I know it."

Horatio began to cough. His coughing soon turned to heaving. He leaned over and vomited nothing but bile into a bucket.

Hardy rushed to his side.

Feeling uncomfortable seeing his father in the weakened state, William hastily said, "Goodbye, Father. I'll stop by tomorrow." William got out of the tent as fast as his legs could take him. The sounds of vomiting kept coming from the tent. It was too much for William to handle. He raced to his horse and rode as fast as he could to the hotel.

CHAPTER FIVE

"When your time comes to die, be not like those whose hearts are filled with fear of death, so that when their time comes they weep and pray for a little more time to live their lives over again in a different way. Sing your death song, and die like a hero going home." – Tecumseh

DEADWOOD CREEK, FIVE MILES OUTSIDE DEADWOOD, DAKOTA TERRITORY

OCTOBER 7, 1876

John leaned against the shovel, admiring the work he, Hans and William had accomplished in the ten days since they had first arrived at the claim. For shelter, they'd built a small shack, large enough for three bunks, a table and a woodstove. To help with prospecting, the slide was completed, and they had dug a new creek bed. Today would be the day they'd break the earthen dam, allowing the water to flow freely, drying out the old bed and giving them fertile ground to dig for gold. However, the gold hadn't been as elusive as they imagined, across several days, they had found small nuggets lying about. This had invigorated William, but something was odd about finding the gold just sitting on top of the ground. Even Hans had mentioned in private to John he was skeptical. The two decided to keep their personal beliefs to themselves. First, because William wouldn't handle it well, and second, they felt it best to keep him in the best of spirits considering Horatio's health had continued to deteriorate.

John had become impressed with William. He might have been born with a silver spoon, but he wasn't afraid of hard work. He wouldn't be exaggerating if he said William worked harder than he and Hans. He was focused and driven, something no doubt his father had instilled in him, but the one weakness William had was his naivety. He mistook bravado for courage, and in a place like Deadwood, that could get a man killed.

"John, come, we need your shovel," William said, waving from the far bank of the creek.

"Be right there," John answered. He waded across the ankle-deep creek and met Hans and William at the earthen dam.

"Gentlemen, today is the day. We've already seen fortune here. Finding the few nuggets we have tells me that beneath that creek bed there, a motherlode could await," William said. "Men, grab your shovels and let's open this up."

All three worked in unison, and within minutes the dam was removed, forcing the Deadwood Creek to flow around the old bed.

Like an excited child, William sprinted to the shack, grabbed a square-head shovel and went to the old creek bed. He began shoveling rocks and dirt into a large pail. "Come, let's get to work."

John and Hans stood and stared past William.

"Men, come, let's get to work," William said. He

finally looked up and saw they were staring at something. He turned around and saw a man on a horse, someone he'd never seen before. He stopped and called out, "Say, can we help you?"

"Are you William Rothman?" the young man asked.

"Why, yes, I am. What can I do for you?" William said.

"Doc sent me. It's about your father," the man replied.

William's face turned white and his stomach tightened. "Yes."

"Doc said you need to come back. It's urgent."

"Urgent how?" William asked, dropping the shovel and heading towards his horse.

"Urgent in that he's dead," the man answered without a tinge of emotion.

William got to his horse but didn't mount it. He leaned against the beast, his right hand on the pommel in a tight grip so he wouldn't collapse.

"Stay here and watch the claim," John ordered Hans.

"Yep," Hans replied.

John ran over to William and said, "Come, let's get you back into town." He gave William a boost to help him onto the horse, then immediately got on Molly.

William didn't say a word. He stared blankly ahead as he followed John back to town.

OUTSKIRTS OF DEADWOOD, DAKOTA TERRITORY

The smell of cooked bacon hit Jimmy's nose, making his mouth water and his stomach growl with hunger. He grabbed two eggs and cracked them. They plopped into the hot bacon grease and began to cook. With a spatula he moved the bacon and flipped the eggs. A show tune came to mind, so he started to hum.

One of the big attractions at the Cricket was the showgirls. They danced and sang to the latest music from New York. Jimmy enjoyed the shows and had Liam put him in charge of directing some of the choreography, not that he was an authority on it, just because he liked to watch the women perform.

Liam had a new saloon and dance hall under construction with a scheduled completion and grand opening set for spring of 1877. The Diamond would be the name, and it would be five times the size of the Cricket, with more women, a larger bar, expanded gaming, a theater, and more rooms for private entertainment. Liam told Jimmy he was to be the manager, a reward for his loyalty.

A crash came from the bedroom.

Jimmy set the spatula down, removed the skillet from the stove top, went to the kitchen table, pulled his Colt, and slowly walked to his closed bedroom door.

Another crash, this time it was glass.

Not wasting a second, Jimmy kicked open the door and entered. He leveled the pistol and said, "I'll shoot you but not to kill. I'll wound you and let you slowly bleed out. Hell, I'll even keep you alive and let you suffer. Now come back in here."

"Why, why are you doing this?" Anna screamed.

"Darlin', crawl back inside and get on the bed like a good girl. I swear I'll wing ya. Your life will be miserable," Jimmy warned.

"It's already miserable. You're a cruel bastard. I hate you!" Anna spat. Blood ran down her right leg from a gash caused by a shard in the window.

"Sweetheart, I've been treating you real good since I brought you here. I've not hurt you, nope. I've fed you, given you nice clothes—"

"Not hurt me? You've raped me every day. You've sodomized me. You're a monster!" she screamed, tears flowing heavily down her reddened cheeks.

The night Sven had been killed by Liam, Jimmy was supposed to go dispose of Anna. When he had arrived at the tent, he couldn't bring himself to do it. Instead he'd kidnapped her and brought her to his house and locked her in his bedroom.

"You can shoot me. I don't care anymore. I'd rather die slowly than live like this anymore," she said and forced herself farther out the window. With each inch she pushed, the glass shard went deeper.

Jimmy sprinted and took her by the arm. He pulled, but she resisted.

"No, let me go!" she screamed.

"Goddamn it!" he said, taking the butt of his pistol and slamming it against the back of her head. The blow knocked her out. He tossed the pistol aside and, using both hands, brought her back inside and laid her on the bed. He ran to the kitchen, took some towels and came back. He pressed the towels against the wound in her leg and applied pressure. He was determined to keep her alive. He couldn't let her die because he'd become obsessed with her.

After stopping the bleeding, he bandaged her leg and secured her to the bed frame, tying each arm and leg to a post. He went to the shed out back, got some spare siding planks and returned to board up the window.

Back in the kitchen, he took the eggs and bacon and plated them. He folded a linen napkin, draped it over his forearm, and went back to the bedroom with the food. There he found Anna awake, her eyes swollen from crying.

She mumbled and groaned beneath the gag he had tied around her head to keep her from screaming.

He sat on the edge of the bed and said, "Are you gonna play nice?"

She tensed her body and let out a muted scream.

"You must be hungry. I made you some eggs and bacon, and this is clean bacon, not from pigs that have eaten human flesh. You have to make sure around here." He laughed.

Her eyes bulged, and she tried to pry her hands free, but the knots around her wrists were tight.

"I'm gonna lower this so you can eat. Promise me you won't yell," he said softly.

She mumbled.

He nestled the plate on his lap and with his left hand reached over and removed the gag.

Not a word exited her mouth.

Taking the fork, he scooped up some egg and gently placed it in her open mouth. "See, that was easy."

She immediately spat the food at him.

Egg and saliva ran down his face. His nostrils flared and his pupils dilated. "I've been nice, so nice, but now I think I need to teach you a lesson. He shoved the gag back in her mouth, put the plate on an end table and removed his suspenders. "I fed Sven to some hogs, yep, three of them. They ate every last piece of him. Even the bone, their teeth and jaws can cut through it like a hot knife cutting through butter." He dropped his pants and crawled on the bed.

Tears burst from her eyes. Her body tensed and she flailed but to no avail.

He looked down at her and said, "That's why you have to make sure you don't eat bacon from Mr. Brown's hogs unless you want some Swedish bacon."

CHAPTER SIX

"The only cure for grief is action." – George Henry
Lewes

YANKTON, DAKOTA TERRITORY

OCTOBER 10, 1876

For John, train stations brought back memories from the
Civil War. He'd never been on a train until the war; his
unit had used one for transport from Atlanta to Virginia,
a courtesy not given when the war ended. The engine was
always an impressive piece of equipment, a modern
marvel, really, he'd thought then. The development of
steam engines hadn't only revolutionized transportation
but had been applied to machines for agriculture. He'd
heard of steam tractors, but they were rarely used and not
by someone like him, a small tenant farmer in Georgia.
The sight and his memories soon gave way to steam
technology that William could use for prospecting. It
would be an idea he'd discuss with him later; now he was
seeing his father's remains were loaded onto the train for
transport back to New York.

John and Hans had escorted William and Horatio's
body to Yankton. The plan from there was to have Hans
take it all the way to New York then return to Deadwood
as soon as possible. This, of course, wasn't what John had
recommended. He'd pressured William to travel with his

father's body and be there for his mother, but William wouldn't have any of it. Hans volunteered to do it, and that was just fine with William.

William had taken the death of his father hard. Since finding out, William hadn't returned to work and had spent the time before the trip to Yankton sequestered in his room.

Grief was something John was familiar with and knew everyone handled it uniquely different. For John, he intended on carrying out Horatio's last wishes until the very end, which was supposed to have been today, according to William's mother, Margaret.

Margaret Rothman had telegrammed William, requesting the remains of Horatio be returned promptly but also called for him to return with it. She was stern in her demand that he return and take over Horatio's position in the company and officially end, as she called it, *'this foolishness in Deadwood'*.

William would hear nothing of it. He'd seen his future, and it was on a separate path than what his father had done. He saw the possibilities and opportunities that Deadwood offered and what his claim could produce, and he was not going to abandon it. He never replied to his mother except to tell her that Horatio's remains were en route and when to expect them to arrive. Knowing his mother well, he wasn't going to give her the heads-up that he wasn't returning. He'd said his goodbyes to Horatio, and deep down, he knew his father would approve. William recalled when his uncle, Horatio's brother, had died. The two were close, and the death affected Horatio, but instead of being lost in grief, Horatio went back to work and carried on. Others questioned his father's behavior, and when asked by William, Horatio calmly and simply said, "Life is for the living." William never forgot those words, and he constantly had them repeating in his head. No, when he finally returned home, he'd come back a conquering hero, a self-made man, something his father would be deeply proud of.

"All aboard!" the conductor cried out.

Hans stuck his hand out to William and said, "I'll take good care of your father. He was always good to me, something I've never forgotten."

William took Hans' hand and firmly shook it. "Thank you. He liked you a lot."

"John, take care, and don't find all the gold while I'm gone," Hans joked, shaking his hand.

"We'll leave you some," John replied. "Be safe."

Hans boarded the train, turned and gave one last wave.

William and John stood until the train left the depot and was out of sight.

"Should we get something to eat?" John asked.

"No, let's ride."

"Hungry for something else," John said with a smile.

"Yes…gold," William answered. He put his hand on John's shoulder and continued, "Let's get back to Deadwood."

DEADWOOD, DAKOTA TERRITORY

Liam enjoyed his morning ritual, a cup of coffee and the *Deadwood Gazette*. He liked to keep tabs on the comings and goings of everyone and everything, and the paper was one tool in his information war. Liam had numerous people working for him; many were typical employees while others were more covert. From the man who worked the livery to the Chinese owner of the town's laundry service, he had them all on payroll to funnel him information. In a place like Deadwood, having information was sometimes the deciding key in negotiations. He didn't leverage it much, but when he had to, he would, and he had no problems being ruthless about it.

One man Liam had on payroll was the Deadwood marshal, Con Stapleton. Don't be confused, Deadwood was still for the most part a lawless town, as Con typically only enforced what little law the town had if the evidence was overwhelming, but for the most part he was an empty suit. After the murder of Wild Bill Hickok, the miners demanded some law and order. They'd first elected Issac Brown, who was subsequently gunned down less than two weeks later outside town. A month later they elected Con to the position.

Con wasn't a lawman by trade, and it showed in how he enforced the law. He was an opportunist and gambler, and one pastime he enjoyed the most was helping Jimmy and Liam organize wrestling and prizefights for entertainment. With Con as the marshal, Liam had his ear and paid him handsomely to feed him critical information.

The front doors swung open, and in sauntered Con, in his wide-brimmed hat one size too big for his head. He marched up to Liam and tapped his knuckles on the bar. "Top of the mornin'," he said in his thick Irish accent. Con had emigrated from Ireland to the United States in 1871.

"Good morning, Marshal, do you want a cup of coffee? It's fresh," Liam asked, lowering the newspaper.

"I will and a wee bit of whiskey in it too if you don't mind," Con said, motioning with his fingers.

"For you, my friend, anything," Liam said, pouring a cup of coffee and filling a shot glass with whiskey.

Con took the glass and poured it into the steaming cup of coffee. He lifted it, inhaled deeply and said, "Ah, may the good Lord always be smiling upon us." He took a large sip and smiled.

"What brings you in here this early?" Liam asked.

"Well, Liam, maybe I'm coming for a social visit," Con said.

"I'm a master at bullshitting, so I know when I'm getting some. Just tell me what's going on," Liam said.

Con took off his hat and smoothed out his matted hair. "How do I put it?" he asked himself.

"Spit it out. I like my information without flowers and perfume."

"I've had some people report they've heard screams and cries coming from Jimmy's house. I dismissed their suspicions and told them Jimmy likes to play rough, if you know what I mean, but I had two more people come this morning," Con said.

"Do these people live next to him?" Liam asked.

"As a matter of fact, yes."

"Then chalk it up to Jimmy having, how would you put it, a wee bit of fun," Liam said.

"You know I thought that too, but being marshal, I have to exercise my due diligence—I don't want people thinking I don't do my duly elected job to the best of my ability—so I stopped by. I knocked, but Jimmy wasn't there..."

"'Cause he's out of town on business for me."

"I didn't go in, but I swear I heard someone in the house."

"So what?"

"Well, they sounded like they were muzzled, if you know what I mean," Con said.

Annoyed with Con's questioning and inquisitive behavior, Liam leaned across the bar and asked, "How much do I pay you to give me information and to look the other way on things?"

"You pay a fair share, that you do," Con answered.

"Then what the hell are you doing in here now? If my man has a harem of women tied up and he's having his way with them every night, do I pay you to snoop on him and tell me about it? No. I pay you to take care of me, and that includes taking care of Jimmy. Do I make myself clear?"

Taken aback, Con's expression went stoic. "Crystal."

"Good, now unless you have something that pertains

to our professional arrangement, kindly drink your coffee and leave!" Liam said.

"Yes, Liam," Con said, cowering.

Con quickly finished his coffee, said his goodbyes and left.

When the door closed, Liam began to wonder just what Jimmy had going on. He trusted Jimmy more than most, but that wasn't saying a lot. What he didn't need was Jimmy drawing attention to himself, which could then draw attention to him. If he had someone tied up, he'd have to see who and why.

CHAPTER SEVEN

"We are like chameleons, we take our hue and the color of our moral character, from those who are around us." – John Locke

DEADWOOD CREEK, FIVE MILES OUTSIDE DEADWOOD, DAKOTA TERRITORY

OCTOBER 12, 1876

Not having Hans working at the claim was noticeable, but it didn't deter William. With his father dead and his mother demanding his return, he had a renewed purpose to see his claim successful.

The excavation of the old creek bed wasn't producing much. They had found flakes but not one nugget.

Needing a break from the continuous hours of labor, the two sat on the bank of the creek, drinking cool water.

Movement across the creek caught John's attention. He focused and saw a small face staring at them behind a fallen tree. "Psst, I think I see that kid."

Looking around, William asked, "Where?"

"Directly across the creek, behind the fallen tree. He's looking right at us."

William spotted the fallen tree and quickly found the boy. "Do you suppose he's hungry?" William asked.

"If he lives out here, yeah, I'm sure he is," John said,

pulling out a piece of hardtack from a satchel next to him. He held it up and waved the hard biscuit.

The boy didn't respond; he only stared.

"Boy, come, are you hungry?" William asked loudly.

Still the boy sat motionless.

John stood up and began to walk towards him. He crossed the creek, but the second he stepped off the embankment, the boy ducked below the rotting tree trunk. "I won't hurt you, I promise. I have some food. I know you must be hungry."

No response.

John stopped his approach when he spotted the boy peering from beneath the fallen trunk. "How about I leave it right here." John placed the hardtack on the ground and stepped away. He crossed back over the creek, turned around, and waited for Jeremiah.

Jeremiah popped his head above the trunk. He gave John a quick look before putting his gaze upon the hardtack.

"Go ahead," John said.

Jeremiah pounced from his concealed position, ran to the biscuit, snatched it, and sprinted back to the cover of the tree.

John cracked a smile and said, "If you want more, just let me know. My name is John, and this is William."

William tipped his hat towards Jeremiah and said, "How do you do, son."

Jeremiah devoured the hardtack and wiped his mouth. He gave John a look and mumbled, "More."

John retrieved another piece from his satchel,

crossed the creek, and held it out for Jeremiah.

Cautious, Jeremiah wouldn't budge. He pointed to the ground and said, "Leave."

"No problem," John said and put it on the ground. He turned and walked away.

Like before, Jeremiah came out, took the hardtack, and went back to the fallen tree.

"Well, if you want more, you'll have to come get it. It's here in my bag," John said, pointing to the satchel on the ground.

Jeremiah looked at him and then towards the bag.

Ready to move on, William wiped his sweaty brow with his sleeve and pondered out loud, "We found nuggets, so there has to be gold here."

The thought brought John back to the situation at hand, finding gold. He wanted to tell William his theory but once more held back. After everything William had been through, the last thing he wanted to do was demoralize him.

"Many people are finding gold in the creek, and why?" William asked.

"'Cause it's floating down from a source, that one claim farther up," John said, referring to the Homestake claim.

"Correct. Now we need to think about geological history. There's been flooding over the years and erosion, right?" William asked, standing up, the tempo of his speech increasing.

"Yeah," John agreed.

"So imagine, if you will, heavy, Biblical rains striking

this area eons ago, tearing away at the source area and forcing the gold to flow. The floods recede, leaving behind the deposits. Now if this part of the creek flooded, where's the natural place deposits would have stayed, virtually protected?" William asked, walking towards the rock outcropping.

Feeling William's excitement, John got to his feet and pointed to the outcropping. "There."

William placed his hands on it and said, "Exactly. We've been looking for flakes when we should be looking for old deposits, large nuggets that flowed down here long ago and got stuck." He raced back and grabbed a shovel. "John, what are we waiting for? Let's start digging."

William's enthusiasm was contagious. John picked up a shovel and bucket and joined him at the base of the outcropping.

Holding his shovel firmly in his hands, William scooped up a pile of stone and dirt and poured it into the bucket.

John followed suit.

The two dug and filled one bucket after another. When one was filled, they'd take it to the slide and dump it.

Hours later they had excavated an area eight feet by twelve feet with a depth of four feet. The slide was piled high and ready to process. John filled the buckets with water and returned so they could begin the process of sifting through the dirt and rocks.

More hours drifted by until the sun slowly retreated

over the mountain to the west.

John was tired and his back sore. "The sun's riding low."

"Let me go through this last bit. Gather our things and ready the horses," William said, his focus on the dirt in the slide.

"A hot bath sounds perfect right now," John said, slowly walking towards the horses.

"Gold," William said just above a whisper. He hurried to a bucket of water and dipped the fist-sized rock into it.

John turned around and watched.

William removed the rock from the water and held it close. "Holy cow, it's gold. John, come look. It's a huge nugget of gold!"

John raced over.

William handed him the huge nugget and said, "That came from the last bucket we hauled out of there. The gold, it's deep, it's deep down near the wall of the outcropping. That's it, that's where we need to dig!"

There was no doubt what John was holding was the largest nugget of gold he'd ever laid eyes on. "You were right."

William embraced John and squeezed tightly. "We did this, we did!"

"It was your idea. It's your claim," John reminded William.

Pulling away, William said, "This is our find. My father taught me years ago that the best person to work alongside isn't hired help but someone who has skin in the game. John Nichols, I hereby declare you ten percent owner of the Rothman claim."

"Ah, are you sure?" John questioned. "Maybe you want to sleep on that."

"No. Not at all. I don't want to do this by myself. I want to do this with a partner. Of course, I'm the majority owner and make the decisions, but you now own ten percent. Is it a deal?"

"I don't know what to say," John said. "That's too generous."

"Say yes," William said, his eyes twinkling with excitement.

John chewed on it longer than any normal person would. He'd received generosity before, but not in this way. People had given him time and care, but not financial generosity on this scale.

"Well?" William asked.

John looked at the nugget in his hand, thought more and said, "Yes."

William threw his arm over John's shoulder and said, "I'll get Mr. Atkins to amend the claim, adding you to it; I'll do the same once Hans returns too. Father would have wanted that."

"I don't know what to say."

"Just say that you'll work this thing until we extract every flake of gold out of this claim," William said.

"I will."

"Good, now let's go celebrate!"

"Sounds good," John said. He grabbed his satchel, but thinking of Jeremiah, he pulled the remaining hardtack and several pieces of jerky out and left them on a stone. He looked towards the fallen tree and said, "Here's dinner. Watch over the claim for us."

Jeremiah peeked over the tree and simply nodded.

DEADWOOD, DAKOTA TERRITORY

After a well-deserved hot bath and dinner, John and William went to get a few celebratory drinks. They exited the hotel, and John naturally turned right to head to the Number Ten Saloon; however, William went left.

"Where are you going?" John called out.

"The Cricket, I want to see the look on Liam Prince's face when I show him this," William said, holding up their find.

"I don't like that place. Let's go to the Ten," John urged.

"You go. I want to see Liam salivate," William said with an arrogant tone. He strutted away, paying no mind to what John wanted.

This was the entitled William John didn't like, but even though they were now technically partners, he still felt an obligation to watch over William. Annoyed, John caught up and said, "Just one drink. Then we head to the Ten."

"Sure," William said.

The two entered the Cricket to find it busier than normal. They pushed their way through the crowds until they found a spot at the bar. There they found Jimmy working the bar.

Jimmy nodded and asked, "Evening, what can I get for you?"

"A bottle," William said.

"You said one drink," John said.

"A bottle is one drink. C'mon, John, lighten up. Enjoy the moment," William said, patting John on his shoulder.

Jimmy brought a full bottle back with two glasses. "That'll be two dollars."

"Two dollars? It was fifty cents the first time we came in here," John complained.

"It was, but on account we have a prizefight tonight, Liam raised the price," Jimmy said, explaining why there were more people than usual.

Begrudgingly, John took the bottle, pulled the cork and poured.

"Two dollars is nothing for us, especially after finding this today," William said, putting the nugget on the bar.

Jimmy's eyes widened, and his mouth hung open. "Where did you get that?"

"At the claim," William said, holding his chest high.

"May I?" Jimmy asked, pointing at the nugget.

"Sure," William said.

John sneered and tossed back his drink.

Jimmy examined the nugget closely and said, "Impressive. I think that's one of the biggest I've ever seen come through here. Will you be needing to have it exchanged?"

Before William could answer, John blurted out, "No.

We do our exchanges at the Barns Hardware store."

William didn't like being interrupted and chimed in, "Depends on the exchange rate."

"Their rate is horrible; plus we can use the exchange at the hardware to get a big credit for supplies and things we'll need to expand the operation at the claim," John countered.

Ignoring John, William asked Jimmy, "Where's Liam? I'd like to see if he'd give us a decent or comparable rate here."

"He's in his office. I'll go fetch him," Jimmy said, heading off without pause.

With Jimmy gone, John turned to William and snapped, "I'm your partner. Yes, I'm only ten percent, but doing business with Prince is wrongheaded."

"I'll remind you, I still retain all rights to make all decisions for the claim, including the liquidation of the ore we find, and might I add that if it were up to you, I wouldn't have gotten the claim. You're too conservative. You need to take more risks," William chided.

John could feel his anger well up. He didn't take too kindly to being treated like a child. He gripped his glass tightly and tossed it back, promptly filled it, and again gulped that down.

"Mr. Rothman, so good to see you," Liam said, walking up, his arms raised in a welcoming gesture.

"Evening, Liam," William said.

"James tells me you made quite a find today," Liam said, putting on his spectacles.

"I did, Liam, and of course I came here first to thank

you for brokering the deal and to see what sort of exchange rate you'll give me," William said.

"Let me see what you have," Liam said.

William handed Liam the nugget.

After holding the gold for a moment, Liam roared, "Eureka!"

"Eureka exactly!" William blared.

"My friend, I'll give you ten percent above my normal cash rate or twenty-five percent above for in-house credit."

John couldn't hold back. "Damn it, William, we don't need booze and whores; we need supplies and equipment."

"But if you need to consult with your employee, please take a moment," Liam said, taking a jab at John.

William shook his head and said, "There's that look."

"What look?" John asked, knowing what it meant but still asking.

"That look that says I'm gonna kill you." William laughed.

"He does have a look, doesn't he?" Liam chimed in, once more jabbing John.

William put his attention back on Liam and said, "I don't need to consult with John, but I'll decline the offer although I do appreciate you extending a special rate for me."

"Are you sure?" Liam asked.

"I'm positive," William said.

Both men locked glares.

Without breaking his, William drank his shot and

slammed the glass down.

A smile broke out across Liam's face. He wasn't used to being defied, but he wasn't about to show William he had gotten to him. "I congratulate you on the find, but if you'll excuse me, I have other business to attend to." He turned and walked off but not before signaling to Jimmy to follow.

Jimmy followed Liam back to his office and closed the door.

"Tell me you left that gold at that cocksucker's claim!" Liam roared.

"I didn't," Jimmy answered.

Liam slammed his fist into his desk. "You're telling me that smug bastard found that there?"

"It appears—"

"I know what it appears to be. Here's what you're going to do. You're going to spend every waking hour watching them. I want to know for sure if that claim is really panning out, and if it is, I want it back."

"You do? Why?"

"'Cause I do."

"I don't think he'll sell if it's paying out," Jimmy said.

Liam swung around and ordered, "I don't care how you do it, but I want that claim back if it's got gold. And do this for me too, make sure that son of a bitch tells the entire town about his find today."

"Yes, sir," Jimmy said.

Another minute passed without a word said between them.

Liam gave Jimmy a hard look and snapped, "What

are you waiting for? Get the hell out of my office and get to work."

Jimmy hurried away.

Back in the bar, John stood fuming over how William had treated him. Not wanting to get into a confrontation, John decided to call it a night. He put his glass down and said, "I'm going back to the hotel room."

William took him by the arm and said, "It was all an act."

"Was it?"

"Yes."

John shrugged his arm away from William's grip and said, "Then next time tell me." John marched off.

"Come back, John. C'mon, we're supposed to be celebrating," William said.

"Liam said drinks on the house for you," Jimmy said, reappearing behind the bar.

William turned, smiled and said, "That's mighty nice. That's one offer I'll accept from Liam."

Jimmy filled William's glass and slid two gold-dollar coins back across the bar, refunding him for the bottle of whiskey. "Do you mind if I see that nugget?"

"Of course," William said, removing it from his pocket and handing it over to Jimmy.

Loudly Jimmy said to several men next to William, "Would you look at that, boys, the Rothman claim is paying out."

The men's eyes grew.

Jimmy turned to the other side of William and attracted those patrons, who in return gave the nugget and William their full attention.

Enjoying the spotlight, William began to boast and promised that today's find was the first in many and he'd be the next Deadwood gold baron.

***

John wasn't finished drinking. He made his way through the rowdy streets until he found himself bellied up at the bar in the Number Ten Saloon.

"Whiskey," John said from behind grinding teeth.

The bartender brought him a glass and a bottle.

John took it and poured.

"You look like you need that," Garrett said from his usual spot at the bar.

John glanced over and replied, "I look that bad?"

Garrett joined him and answered, "Yes, you do."

"Any breaks in your case?" John asked, already knowing the answer.

"Same as before," Garrett said. "South Carolina?"

"Huh?" John said.

"Where you're from?"

"Georgia, outside Atlanta," John said.

"I'm a Virginia man. Fought with Lee at Fredericksburg," Garrett said.

"Me too, small world," John said.

The two shared their common war experiences, with Garrett growing more agitated as he detailed his capture at Petersburg.

"The one fortunate thing...the war ended right after.

I was released soon after," Garrett said then took a drink.

"It was all a waste," John said.

"You believe that?" Garrett asked.

"I do. What did we gain from it?

"I hear what you mean," Garrett said. He had some different thoughts but avoided challenging John's bitter assessment and instead focused on more personal questions. "What brings you to Deadwood?"

"I'm surprised you don't know already, being a Pinkerton," John quipped.

Garrett laughed and said, "I did ask about you. Heard you were hired security, is that true?"

"It is," John answered.

"No wife or children?"

"Is this an interrogation, or are you just making conversation?" John asked.

"Making conversation," Garrett replied.

"I'll give you the abridged version. Went home to Georgia; found my wife and daughter had been murdered. Spent the next eleven years tracking down their killers. Worked as assistant deputy marshal in Dodge City before being hired to come here."

"Oh, you were a lawman?" Garrett asked.

"Not for long, this job was more lucrative," John said.

"Ever thought of applying to the Pinkertons?"

"Never."

"Well, when this job ends, please do. The agency could use more Southern blood. There's not many of us," Garrett said, tossing back his shot. He picked up his hat and continued, "I'm leaving in a few days. I've been given orders to report to St. Joseph, Missouri, a new assignment."

"Oh yeah, what is it?"

"Sorry, that's confidential," Garrett said, holding out his hand. "Nice meeting you. Always good to chat with a soldier of Dixie."

John shook his hand and said, "Have a good life."

Garrett waved goodbye to the bartender and exited the saloon.

With Garrett gone, John's thoughts quickly returned to his last contact with William. In order for him to forget the sting, he'd have to soothe it with a few more drinks.

CHAPTER EIGHT

"It was pride that changed angels into devils; it is humility that makes men as angels." – Saint Augustine

DEADWOOD, DAKOTA TERRITORY

OCTOBER 13, 1876

John stared at his plate of eggs and grits. Normally William would be sitting across from him in the busy hotel restaurant, but this morning was different. It wasn't like William to run late, so his no-show was beginning to concern John.

After breakfast, John proceeded to William's room and knocked.

No answer.

He entered the room to find it empty, only adding to his worry.

John went to the front desk. "Have you seen Mr. Rothman?"

"No, sir, I haven't seen Mr. Rothman all morning," the clerk replied.

There was only one place to go, and that was the last place he'd seen William, the Cricket. John raced from the hotel, his gun belt on, and made his way towards the Cricket with purpose in his step. He burst through the entrance of the bar to find it sparsely occupied. At the bar he saw Liam leaning over a newspaper, reading. "Where is he?" John asked from across the bar.

Liam looked up and cocked his head. "You enter my establishment looking like you want a fight and asking me questions that I don't know the answer to."

"Where is he?" John again asked. Now only a couple of feet separated the two men.

"I presume you're inquiring about your employer," Liam replied smugly, folding the paper.

"Where is William?" John asked.

"I sense anger and, I daresay, a tinge of disrespect in your tone. If I weren't a moderate man, I'd say you're making an accusation of some sort. Many men wouldn't allow someone to make wild accusations, but alas, I'm not many men, and I'll excuse your ill-tempered accusations this one time."

John put his hand on the back strap of his pistol. "Where is he?"

"You come into my place making accusations in such a tone, and now you threaten me?" Liam said, his spine growing tall.

"John, what are you doing?" William asked from the second-floor balcony.

Looking up, John saw William putting on his suspenders. "You weren't at breakfast."

"I know, 'cause I was here," William answered.

"I went to your room. I looked around," John said.

"What's gotten into you?" William asked, slowly walking down the stairs.

"I just thought—"

"You thought wrong, and next time you come into

my place acting this way, you'll exit on your back," Liam growled.

John tightened his jaw after hearing Liam's words.

"Did you threaten Liam?" William asked.

"I was looking for you. I thought something had happened to you," John said.

"Your man owes me an apology," Liam said, taunting John.

"Maybe Liam is right," William said.

Not able to suffer William's condescension again, John snapped, "Are we doing this again? I'm not playing this game again."

"John, you came into his establishment making accusations. Did you ever think to simply ask if he'd seen me?" William said.

"I did ask," John said.

"If that's asking, I'm the pope," Liam quipped.

"Shut your mouth," John snapped, his jaw clenched.

Liam cut his eyes then turned to William. "I suggest you remove your employee before something very bad happens to him."

John squared off with Liam.

Liam removed his hands from the bar and lowered them to grab the shotgun he had hidden below the bar.

William stepped in between both men and faced John. "I think you and I need to go…now."

John didn't reply.

"You're a smart man. Get him out of here," Liam said.

The sound of a door opening to the far right of the

bar drew William's attention. There stood Jimmy and Oliver, both holding rifles. "John, this is a fight you won't win. Let's go."

John removed his hand from the back strap of his pistol and relaxed his stance.

William turned and said, "Thank you for a wonderful night."

"You're very welcome. We look forward to having you back, minus your ill-tempered employee."

William nudged John along until they exited the bar. "What are you doing?"

"I was looking for you, and that son of a bitch can't be trusted," John answered.

"You keep telling me that," William said. "Come, let's go back to the hotel; then we'll head off to the claim."

The two men walked off.

The doors of the Cricket opened. Liam and Jimmy stepped out. They watched William and John disappear into the crowded street.

"Make sure you kill that cocksucker slowly."

"It will be my pleasure," Jimmy said.

NEW YORK, NEW YORK

Margaret Rothman touched Horatio's cold hand even though the undertaker told her it wasn't advisable. It had been months since she'd seen her husband, and if this was going to be the last time she'd touch his skin, then nothing was going to stop her.

Memories of all their years came crashing back, from the first time they met at a cocktail party for the mayor until the day he and William departed for their adventure out West.

She had protested the journey, but her words fell flat. For Horatio, he saw the experience as a way to turn William into the man who could rightfully take his place at the head of his company, and for William, it was a way for him to prove to his father he was more than the boy so many said he was.

Regardless of the virtues the trip promised, Margaret felt it was too dangerous, and now she stood above proof positive that she was right.

When she'd received the telegram from William concerning Horatio's illness, she knew; she just knew it would be the one thing that would take down such a powerful and impressive man.

Longingly she waited for the train to arrive with Horatio's remains, knowing that William would be there too, but when she discovered he wasn't, her heart melted. Not only had she lost her beloved husband, but she was losing her only son. The allure of the West was calling, and he was heeding it.

However, what William didn't know was where she lacked the business prowess of Horatio, she excelled in getting what she wanted, regardless of the obstacles. He might have disregarded her plea to come home, but could he say no if she were standing there in front of him?

"Mrs. Rothman, Rabbi Abrams has arrived; he'd like a word before the service," Michael, the funeral home director, said.

"Yes, thank you, and, Mr. Wallace, thank you for allowing me to see him...like this," Margaret said, nodding towards Horatio's body.

"Of course, ma'am," Michael said. He turned and opened the door for her.

Margaret exited the back room and into a long hallway lit by four candlelit sconces. She gingerly walked down the hall until it ended, and entered a large room. The room would be where the service would be held. In the far corner a man was admiring the large flower arrangements.

"Rabbi Abrams, how do you do?" Margaret said, walking towards him.

Abrams turned and quickly closed the distance between the two. "How are you, Margaret?"

"I'm making do, thank you," she answered.

"Good, glad to hear it. I went ahead and wrote something that I wanted to share with you," he said, handing her a sheet of paper.

She took it and began to read.

"I noticed the flowers. Will these be here? Traditionally, there aren't flowers at a Jewish funeral," Abrams said.

She finished reading and said, "This is fine, and as far as the flowers go, I'm permitting them. Horatio had many friends; most weren't Jewish. If I turned them away, I'd fear they'd take offense." Ensuring the funeral was as inclusive as possible was more important to her than sticking to strict Jewish guidelines. While they were

Jewish, they didn't practice the religion with vigor. For her, she wanted the affair to honor her husband more than honor her God.

"Of course," Abrams said. "Do you approve of everything I wrote and who I suggest to come do the readings?"

"Yes," she answered.

A man entered the room, catching her eye. She looked and saw it was Hans. "Rabbi, if you'll excuse me, I need to see this gentleman."

"But, Mrs. Rothman, do you need me to go over any other specifics?" Abrams asked.

"Rabbi, I'm quite confident in your abilities. I trust you'll make the appropriate choices," she said and walked off to meet Hans.

"Good day, Mrs. Rothman," Hans said.

"I'm glad you're here," she said.

"Of course, I wouldn't be anywhere else. Your husband was like a father to me. He gave me an opportunity when few would," Hans said.

"Yes, I know, and he cared for you, more than you might know. I also wanted to thank you personally for bringing him back. I know I must have seemed rude at the train station when you arrived with his remains, but I have to say that was shock at discovering it was you and not William."

"He wanted to come, I can assure you," Hans lied, hoping to ease any pain she might have felt from William not returning.

"He did? Then why not come? I don't understand

what's gotten into him," she complained.

"Ma'am, do you mind if I'm candid?" Hans asked.

"Please be."

"He's in love. There's no other way to say it…"

"What's her name? Who is she?" Margaret huffed.

"Deadwood is her name," Hans confessed.

"I don't understand."

"The camp, the bars, the prospecting, the people, John, all of it—he's in love with the experience. It's become intoxicating to him, I think."

"He'd rather stay there and play cowboy than come home with his father's body? What's gotten into him? The level of disrespect is unparalleled."

"When I return, shall I convey a message from you?" Hans asked.

"Who's this John?"

"He's the hired muscle. A former confederate soldier and deputy marshal we met in Dodge City. He's a gunslinger, to be more accurate. William thinks highly of him, and I believe he wants to impress him," Hans answered.

"Impress him, a Southern ruffian, a rebel? He stays for him and not his own father, not his mother?"

"Ma'am, I don't think that's the sole reason. The claim has potential. I believe William wants to make a name for himself."

Margaret stewed on what Hans had just told her.

"Let me know what I can convey to him, or if there's a letter you'd like me to deliver, I can do that as well," Hans said.

"I have a big favor to ask of you," Margaret said nervously.

"Of course, anything."

"When do you leave to go back to Deadwood?" she asked.

"I leave on the train tonight, ma'am," Hans answered.

She looked over her shoulder and saw Abrams pacing and reciting. "There's still a little over an hour before the funeral begins, so I need you to leave and go to the train station."

Interrupting her, he asked, "Now? What for?"

"I need you to procure me a ticket. I'm coming to Deadwood with you."

DEADWOOD, DAKOTA TERRITORY

Tired after a long day watching William and John pull more gold from their claim, Jimmy returned to his house first before reporting to Liam.

He entered the darkened house, lit an oil lamp, and headed directly for his bedroom. He unlocked the door and entered.

The glow of the lamp scattered the dark and illuminated the horrors inside.

Anna was tied to the bed, as she had been since the day she escaped. Her wrists and ankles were raw and bleeding. The remaining parts of her exposed skin were covered in bruises. Her gaunt face showed the signs of abuse and malnutrition. Her deep blue eyes were sunken, and her hair was thin and oily.

When Jimmy approached, she no longer fought. What defiance she had shown before was gone, a casualty of Jimmy's torture.

Jimmy removed her gag and said, "Evening, sweetheart."

Anna didn't reply; she only stared at the ceiling.

He set the oil lamp down and removed his gun belt. "I'm tired. Ole Liam has me watching that rich kid's claim. Liam ain't gonna like it when I tell him he's pulled even more gold from it," Jimmy said, pulling off his boots.

Anna still lay motionless and silent.

"I'll tell you, Liam, he's a hard-ass, wants me to get that claim back, and I know what that means. That'll mean I'll have to kill them," Jimmy said with a sigh. "I just want a quiet life, with you by my side, but until then I need to keep doing what I need to do. Thing is, Liam, he acts like he's so smart, but most of his ideas are mine. He had me get that rich kid drunk last night so he'd boast and talk. That was my idea. That's what I did to—" Jimmy said but stopped short of saying Sven's name. "Liam frustrates me. He takes credit for every good idea I put forth. You know I could take Liam's place and do a better job of it. What do you think? Should I just get rid of Liam instead?"

Anna shuddered.

Jimmy gave her a look and continued, "Or maybe we should just leave. How does California sound? I hear the ocean is a wonderful sight. Waves so big, they're as tall as any man. Can you believe it, a wave as tall as a man?" He stood and removed his pants.

Upon hearing his pants hit the floor, tears welled in Anna's eyes, as she knew what was coming next.

He sat on the edge of the bed and caressed her thigh. "I missed you today." He paused and continued, "I know that me holding you like this isn't nice and all, but soon you'll come to love me too, and when that happens, I'll untie you."

Tears streamed down her cheeks.

"I can't stay long. I have to head to the Cricket and give Liam a report on Rothman," he said, getting on top of her.

She grunted in pain as he placed his weight fully on top of her.

He finished quickly, got up and went to the washbasin across the room. "I need you to eat, so when I come back later, I'll cook up some of them taters I got and the pork belly."

Anna just lay silent, her tears dry.

Jimmy got dressed, walked to the bedside, put the gag back in her mouth and said, "I'll miss you when I'm gone." He touched her hair and said, "How about I give you a bath tonight, huh?"

Still Anna remained quiet.

He leaned down and kissed her forehead. "I love you."

All Anna could do was think about killing him. She prayed for the opportunity, but Jimmy was careful, and not since that day she'd attempted to escape had he left her untied.

Jimmy stopped at the door and turned. "I'll be back soon, I promise."

***

Liam paced his office as the words of William's continued success spilled out of Jimmy's mouth. *Has William found another source? Why is there so much gold in one place? Is it how they're prospecting?* He had many questions, but one thought kept coming back: he wanted that claim and now.

"So it appears that claim isn't played out at all," Jimmy said.

"Where are they finding it?" Liam asked.

"They're digging at the base of a rock outcropping near the far end of the claim," Jimmy answered.

Hoots and hollering vibrated through the thin walls from the bar below.

"There's no time to waste. Do what you need to do, but get me that claim back as soon as possible," Liam ordered.

"Okay, I'll take care of them as soon as possible," Jimmy said, his mind processing the various ways he'd do it.

"Good," Liam said.

Jimmy stood waiting for Liam to say something else.

"Don't just stand there. Go make it happen. The next time I see you, I want them both gone," Liam snarled.

Without hesitation, Jimmy turned and exited, leaving Liam again pacing his small office.

CHAPTER NINE

"A gem cannot be polished without friction, nor a man perfected without trials." – Lucius Annaeus Seneca

TWO MILES OUTSIDE DEADWOOD, DAKOTA TERRITORY

OCTOBER 14, 1876

The sun's early light gradually illuminated the long stretches of the trail. Whatever had gotten into William the night before was gone; his verbose hubris had melted away, replaced with humility. After the hard work yesterday, he and John had finished and gone back to the hotel to clean up and rest.

John couldn't stop thinking about how he'd been treated by William, and inside, he was holding a deep resentment that needed to be properly processed.

"John, I wanted to again apologize for my behavior the other night. I was inappropriate and I belittled you. I promise that you won't see such as that again," William said.

John gripped the reins of Molly tight as he pondered how to properly respond. He appreciated the apology, but he needed to make it clear he'd not tolerate the way William treated him again.

"Nothing to say?" William asked.

John clenched his jaw and finally spit out his

thoughts. "Your apology is heard and accepted, but you need to know that if you truly intend on making me a partner, being that it's only ten percent, I won't hear such words again."

"I meant what I said about the stake in the claim. I just didn't have time yesterday, as you well know. I'll get it handled later today, I promise," William said, referring to adding John to the title of the claim.

"I believe you, and even if I weren't a partner, I won't be talked to like that. I've done and seen too much to be treated like a common servant," John declared.

"I hear you and I respect you," William said.

"Good."

"About the claim, word has gotten out. I think one of us needs to start staying out there from now on. We can take shifts."

"I do tonight, then," John said.

"Fair enough. That'll give me time to get the title handled with the lawyer later, then," William said.

The two turned down a part of the trail that William disliked due to the narrow path and edge that doglegged the side of the steep hill.

"We need to reconnoiter a new way to get to our claim. I hate this damn trail," William said, looking to his left and down the hill that sloped towards the creek below.

Looking over his shoulder, John joked, "Is someone scared of heights?"

"No, just that I don't trust this horse," William answered.

"Then give him a name. Horses like names; helps build trust," John said in jest.

"They do?"

"That's what I've heard," John said with a chuckle.

"Harold? Does he look like a Harold?" William said, rubbing the horse's neck.

"Yeah, that's a good name." John laughed.

Molly neighed and became jittery.

"What is it, girl?" John said, pulling back on her reins. He began to scan the trail in front of them but saw nothing out of sorts.

"Why are you stopping?" William asked, looking down the steep hill.

"Ssh," John snapped, holding his left hand high, signaling for William to be quiet.

Noticing John was concerned, William grew tense. He too began to search the hillside above for anything out of the ordinary.

An eerie quiet settled over them and the surrounding area.

A chill ran up John's spine. He could feel eyes with evil intent fixed on him. He let go of Molly's reins and reached for his Colt.

Footfalls and crashing came from the right of them.

John pulled his Colt and held it firmly.

Jeremiah burst from the tree line, stopped on the trail, and yelled as he waved his arms wildly, "Go. Bad men!"

Gunfire erupted from somewhere above and rained down on John and Molly.

John pivoted to engage but not before Molly was struck several times, once in the hindquarters and twice in the stomach. She lurched forward but lost her footing and fell to the left and off the trail. John attempted to get free from the stirrups but couldn't in time and went with her down the hill. They toppled several times, her weight landing on his left leg briefly before rolling off. John tried to rise, but vertigo set in, and soon a darkness overcame him. Within seconds he was unconscious.

Jeremiah disappeared as quickly as he'd appeared, sprinting downhill away from the gunfire.

More shots came from the hillside. This time William was their intended target.

Scared, William boggled trying to get his pistol; he dropped it on the ground. Terrified, he did what came naturally and tried to flee; however, his attempt was too late. A round struck him in the shoulder and one sliced through the back of his neck, severing his spinal cord. His body went limp and fell off the horse and rolled down the hillside below, resting on a trail farther down. As he lay on the trail, he stared towards the blue cloudless sky. With each breath he took, blood gurgled and spewed from his lips. Thoughts of his life rushed through his mind. He wanted to move but couldn't; he was paralyzed. What he could do was still blink and hear. Sounds of men talking came from above. He couldn't make out who they were or if they were coming. Other noises then came. It was men hollering, but this time from below, near the creek. The last thing William heard before closing his eyes for the last time was the distinct crack of gunfire.

***

"Mister, you okay?" a man said, kneeling next to John.

John opened his eyes but quickly closed them due to the bright sunlight.

"He's alive," the man who went by the name Grant said, excited to see John move.

John shifted his weight but stopped when a stabbing pain shot up from his leg and into his lower back like an electrical shock.

"Here, let me help you," Grant said, taking John's arm and pulling him into a seated position.

John slowly opened his eyes, blinking several times to adjust to the light. "William, where's William?"

Grant, a miner from a claim just below, looked to his two colleagues and said, "He must be referring to the other man." He motioned with his head to the left.

"Where's William?" John asked, struggling to stand.

"Look, mister, you need to rest. You took quite a spill down the hill," Grant said.

John grabbed Grant firmly and asked, "Have you seen William?"

"I don't know how to tell you, so I'll just tell ya. There's another fella over there, and he's dead, shot through the neck," Grant said.

John looked past the man and saw William's body lying face up on the trail, a pool of blood around him. He sighed loudly and shook his head in disgust. He took a step to go to William's side when Molly whined in pain. John looked down the hill farther and spotted her. She lay motionless except for her head lifting up and down. John's heart melted. He made his way to her and knelt next to her and began to pet her head. "Oh girl, I'm so sorry."

The miners followed him down. Grant could feel John's sorrow. "She's hurt real bad."

Knowing what he had to do, John reached for his Colt, but found his holster empty. "Shit."

Grant pulled a Winchester from his belt and handed it to John.

John took the pistol, cocked it and placed the muzzle against Molly's head.

She looked at him.

Her look told John that she was in intense pain. The last thing he wanted to do was kill the one living thing that he had such a connection with for so many years, but there wasn't an option. "I'm so sorry, girl." Not hesitating longer, he pulled the trigger and gasped from the experience. Distraught but also thankful to be alive, he handed the pistol back to Grant and got to his feet. His leg was hurting badly, but somehow he'd managed to survive the encounter uninjured. He pushed past the miners and went to William's side.

Grant followed him and said, "I've got a wagon below. We'll bring it up and help you take your friend into town."

"Thank you," John replied.

"Any idea who might have done this?" Grant asked.

"Possibly, but what I do know is someone saw them," John said.

"Oh yeah?" Grant said.

Not wanting to share this information, John kept it to himself. "That wagon is much appreciated."

"We'll go get it now," Grant said, walking away with his two colleagues.

John looked around, hoping to spot Jeremiah. He was the one person who could lead him to finding who killed William and Molly.

DEADWOOD, DAKOTA TERRITORY

Liam pressed the pistol firmly against Jimmy's head and cocked it.

Quivering in fear, Jimmy knelt, his lip bleeding from the punch Liam had delivered just moments ago. "Please, Liam, I'll find the boy, I promise."

"You said you were going to take care of this, and now it appears it might have gotten worse. I should blow your brains out," Liam sneered with his finger pressed against the trigger.

"We would have gone looking for him, but the little shit ran off and 'cause—"

"'Cause what? Finish your thought," Liam said, jamming the muzzle harder into Jimmy's forehead.

"On account that some miners below heard the shots and started up towards the commotion," Jimmy answered.

"You thought it best to carry this out in the middle of the morning? Why not sneak into their hotel rooms and slit their throats or anything else but what you've done," Liam roared.

"Please, Liam. How was I to know the boy would be there and warn them, or that the miners would respond right away?" Jimmy said, stuttering.

"Planning, you're supposed to think things through. Now your mess up might have exposed us all. First you leave Nichols alive, and that boy saw you…all of you. He can name you or pull you out of a line of people."

"But…but isn't that why we have Con on the payroll? He won't do that; he'll help cover this up. Thing is, road agents are everywhere. Getting attacked on the side of a trail or road isn't uncommon," Jimmy said, hoping he could reason with Liam to let him live.

"There's a damn witness. If that boy talks and says you're involved, that will lead them to me, and I don't want people sniffing around here," Liam snapped.

"I'll fix this, Liam, I swear. Please, let me fix this," Jimmy begged.

"Who helped you with—" A knock on Liam's office door interrupted him. "Who is it?"

"Oliver, sir."

"Go away!"

"Sir, there's a man downstairs. Wants to see you."

"Who the hell is it?" Liam asked, still holding the pistol to Jimmy's head.

"Um, I…I think it's the marshal, sir," Oliver said.

"Well, why didn't you say so," Liam barked, uncocking the pistol and placing it on his desk. "Today is your lucky day. Gather your men and go find that boy. Next time I see you, I better hear good news."

Jimmy sprang to his feet and headed for the door. "Yes, Liam. Only good news next time."

Liam straightened his clothes and followed closely behind Jimmy. He proceeded downstairs to find Con Stapleton leaning against the bar.

The crowd in the bar was picking up, and soon it would be packed, wall to wall, with miners coming from their claims with gold to sell and whiskey to drink.

"Marshal Stapleton, why do I have the honor of your presence?" Liam asked, stepping around the bar and standing in front of Con. He smoothed out his hair and said, "Please tell me this is a social call."

Con's face showed he was stressed. His brow was furrowed and his jaw clenched tight.

Liam grabbed a glass and a bottle of whiskey and placed them in front of Con.

"None for me," Con said, waving his hand.

Liam pinched the bridge of his nose and sighed. "Now what?" Concern grew inside him as he speculated it had to do with William's murder.

"You might have heard William Rothman and John Nichols were attacked on the northeast trail a few miles outside town. Unfortunately, Mr. Rothman didn't survive the attack; however, Mr. Nichols did. I've just spoken with him, and when asked who he thought might have been behind the incident, your name was mentioned," Con replied.

"Me? I can't imagine why," Liam said, acting shocked by the accusation.

"Can we go into your office?" Con asked, his tone

unlike what Liam had seen before. He was serious and seemed determined to get a real answer.

"Of course, follow me," Liam said.

Liam led Con to his office and, once inside, closed the door. He went to his chair and sat down. "So Mr. Rothman is dead?"

Con took the seat in front of the desk, a worn armless oak chair. He held his wide-brimmed hat in his hand, rubbing his thumb along the edge. It was evident he was nervous, yet he pressed on. "Did you have anything to do with this?"

Liam sat up and asked, "Are you asking as the marshal or someone on my payroll?"

"As the marshal of this camp with the legal authority to enforce the laws against crimes such as murder," Con sternly replied.

"My answer is the same no matter what. I didn't have anything to do with Mr. Rothman's death. Now, Marshal, you know there are any number of road agents out there that prey upon hapless victims coming and going from Deadwood."

"I'm aware," Con said.

"And let me add that I'm not sure why Mr. Nichols would mention my name. He doesn't appear to like me, and once again he's accusing me of something nefarious."

"Once again?" Con asked, unaware of the other day.

"Yes, Mr. Nichols barged into the bar the other morning and all but accused me of abducting Mr. Rothman, who had spent the night with one of my women. He stood right down there, hand on his pistol, ready to shoot me if I twitched or scratched an itch."

"He did?" Con asked.

"You can ask Jimmy, Oliver—hell, there were more than a few people in that morning who were witnesses to this."

"Interesting."

"Outside of this fraudulent accusation, is there anyone else?" Liam asked again, leaning back in the chair and putting his feet on the desk.

"It could be the Pelly Gang, but we haven't heard from them since July. I heard they went south, but I suppose it's not out of the realm of possibility they're back. The only thing is no one was robbed."

"Are there any witnesses to this ambush?" Liam asked.

"Yes, the wildling boy that lives out there, and three miners saw the attack but didn't see the attackers."

"Marshal, if you have a witness, you best go find that boy. Any idea where he might be?" Liam asked.

"Mr. Nichols said he'd seem him near their claim a lot. I'm heading out in an hour with a couple of people to go find him."

"Who's going with you? Do you need additional riders? I can help."

"A man named Wyatt Earp and his brother Morgan are going out with me, as well as Mr. Nichols, and I don't think it's best you or your people accompany me," Con answered.

"I understand the delicate nature of this."

Con stood and said, "I best get going. Thank you for

your time."

Liam got up and went to the door and opened it. "Always my pleasure, Marshal."

Con exited but stopped and turned. "I didn't mention they were ambushed, I merely said they were attacked."

Shock washed over Liam. He stared at Con, thought quickly and answered, "Yeah, you did, downstairs; you said ambush."

Raising his right brow, Con tried to recall but couldn't. "I did?"

"Yes, yes, you did."

Con rubbed his face with his right hand and said, "Maybe I did. God, I'm so tired. Why did you suggest I take this position?"

Liam planted his hand on Con's shoulder and answered, "'Cause I couldn't imagine a better man for the job than you."

"Thank you. Well, I better be off," Con said and marched off.

Liam closed his office door, clenched his fist and slammed it onto the desk. The chances of Con and his posse running into Jimmy and his men out at the claim was high. Liam needed to warn Jimmy, 'cause if the two came across each other in the dark of night, things could go sideways fast.

***

Liam pushed and shoved his way through the bustling

streets of town until he reached his destination, Jimmy's house. He had hoped to catch him there before he left, but after knocking more than five minutes with no response, he knew he'd missed him.

The thought of both groups clashing stressed Liam, but his options were limited now. Unable to stop Jimmy from heading out; he needed a fallback plan, something that could get him out of this bind if Jimmy was implicated. Often Liam had insurance policies on people, but there wasn't one he had on Jimmy, at least not to the extent that would prevent him from fingering Liam as an accomplice in William's murder.

Frustrated, Liam sat on the front porch stairs and pondered what he could do. Many ideas swam through his mind, but none would save him if the worst happened. There had to be something. Suddenly something came, he wasn't sure if it was enough, but he was going to find out. He jumped to his feet and tested to see if the door was unlocked; surprisingly, it was. He turned the handle and pushed it open. What little light there was coming from the torches and lanterns in the street penetrated the dark room. Cautiously he entered. He'd never been to Jimmy's house before, so he could only guess where everything was. He headed for a table and found a candle; next to it a box of matches sat. He struck a match; the orange glow lit the room. He lit the wick of the candle, and in seconds the room came into view.

The house was small. A front room, where he now stood, the kitchen and a single door, which had to be the bedroom. He looked around for anything that could prove helpful but saw nothing. He marched directly to the bedroom, turned the nob and pushed it open. A pungent odor wafted over him. "Argh!" he said, recoiling from the smell. He pulled a handkerchief from his pocket, put it to his nose, and entered. When the candle's light washed away the darkness, it exposed Jimmy's dark secret…Anna.

She was tied to the bed, and her health had deteriorated.

"Well, what do you know," Liam said as a smile slid across his face.

Anna slowly turned her head. Her eyes widened when they looked upon Liam standing there.

Liam walked over and sat on the edge of the bed. "Anna?"

She nodded.

"Has he had you in here since Sven disappeared?" Liam asked.

Again she nodded.

"My name is Liam …" he said but stopped when she reacted negatively to hearing his name. "I'm not here to hurt you; on the contrary, I'm here to help."

Tears ran down her hollow cheeks.

"Would you like me to free you? Hmm, would you like that?"

She mumbled, but it was unintelligible due to the gag in her mouth.

Liam removed the gag and asked again, "Would you like me to free you?"

"Yes…please," she answered.

"I'm going to help you, but I need you to help me too. Can you do that?"

"Don't hurt me, please," she begged.

"I'm not here to do that. No, I'm here to help. I'm not like Jimmy, not at all. I'm here to help you, but I need to know that in exchange you'll help me with something," he said, gently rubbing her arm.

"Just don't hurt me, no more, please," she said.

"So you'll help me?"

"Yes, just get me out of here."

Liam pulled a knife from his boot and held it up. The light from the candle glinted off the blade.

More tears poured down her face, her lips quivered, and she moaned, "No, please don't hurt me."

He reached above her head and cut the bindings. He did this for all of them and pocketed the knife. He bent down, scooped her up, and lifted her from the soiled bed. "I won't hurt you. I'm one of the good guys, I swear," he said and headed out the door with her cradled in his arms.

CHAPTER TEN

"Victorious warriors win first and then go to war, while defeated warriors go to war first and then seek to win." – Sun Tzu

DEADWOOD, DAKOTA TERRITORY

OCTOBER 17, 1876

After spending three entire days unsuccessfully looking for Jeremiah, John returned to the hotel. His body ached, and the leg Molly had landed on was hurting badly. It was deeply bruised but didn't seem broken. The morning sun felt good on his face as he dismounted his horse and handed the reins to the livery hand.

"You're lookin' whooped," Steffen, the livery worker said, taking the reins.

"Was out all night. Yes, I'm whooped," John said and walked off. Paying no mind to his surroundings, John entered the hotel and slowly strolled past the front desk clerk.

"Excuse me, Mr. Nichols," Byron, the clerk, said, clearing his throat.

John paused. Without looking at Byron, he replied, "Yes?"

"Sir, your colleague Hans has returned and requested you meet him as soon as possible," Byron said.

"Where is he?" John asked.

"He's having breakfast in the restaurant," Byron said, pointing. "And I didn't tell him about Mr. Rothman. I didn't think it my place."

All John wanted to do was go to sleep, but informing Hans of what had happened to William was critical. "Thank you," John said and headed towards the dining room.

Hans looked up and saw John enter. "John, here."

John glanced and saw Hans waving, but what he wasn't expecting to see was someone at the table with him, a woman. He made his way to the table but didn't sit down. "We need to talk."

"Then sit down. Order the griddle cakes. They're very good," Hans said, smiling.

Margaret cleared her throat.

A look of embarrassment swept over Hans' face. "Oh my, forgive me. John, this is Margaret Rothman. Margaret, this is John Nichols, the man I told you about."

Margaret pursed her lips and said, "So you're the rebel Hans has told me about."

John felt like someone strapped a hundred-pound pack to his back when he heard the woman was William's mother. He stood unsure of how to proceed.

Hans looked down, embarrassed at how Margaret had received John.

John snapped out of his shock and replied, "Rebel? I've been called that before. I'm not sure in what context you're using it now, ma'am."

"Please sit down and join us for breakfast," Hans said.

"I, um…" John said but cut himself off.

"Are you going to sit or just hover?" Hans asked, a look of concern washing over him.

Thoughts of how he'd tell her about William's demise spun through his mind.

"Where's William? I so want to see him," Margaret said.

"Ma'am, can we go somewhere private and talk?" John asked.

"Why? Is something wrong?" Margaret asked.

"John, what's happened?" Hans blurted out.

"If we could go to my room, please. This is not the place to talk," John said calmly.

"You're scaring me. Where's William? Has something awful happened to my boy?" Margaret asked, her voice beginning to crack.

Several surrounding tables picked up on the tense conversation and grew quiet. John noticed and turned to each. "Mind your business."

Hans sprang up and went to Margaret's side. He held out his arm and said, "Ma'am, let me escort you."

Margaret took his arm, her body trembling.

John assisted as well and walked her up the stairs and to his room. They sat her in a cushioned chair and got her a glass of cool water.

Margaret took a drink and removed her hat. When she regained her composure, she asked again, "Where's William?"

John looked her squarely in the eyes and answered, "William is dead. He was murdered."

Her face contorted, and tears burst from her eyes. "No, tell me this is a nightmare, please."

"What happened?" Hans asked.

John replied, "We were ambushed over three days ago on our way to the claim."

"By who?" Hans asked.

"I don't know. I have suspicions," John replied.

Margaret's sobbing brought Hans to her side. "Ma'am, maybe you should go to your room and lie down."

She pushed Hans away and snapped, "I don't want to lie down. I want to know where my boy is. Mr. Nichols, where is his body?"

Unsure how to properly answer, he told her the truth. "I have it stored on ice at McCallester's."

"Is that a funeral home?" she asked.

"Not exactly," John answered.

"Then what is it?" she asked.

"It's an ice house."

"An ice house? Why has his body not been treated properly?" she roared with anger. "Why wasn't I informed of his death?"

"I sent a wire back to New York," John replied.

Ignoring John, Margaret continued to rail against him. "Is this how you respect the dead here? You put them on ice?"

Understanding her anger was stemming from deep pain, John chose not to let her stinging comments hurt him. "I sent a wire. I never received a reply. In the meantime I have been attempting to find out who killed your son and bring them to justice."

"Where is he? I want to see him, now!" Margaret hollered as she stood up.

"I'll take you there, but can I ask you to calm down?" John said.

Hearing this, Hans shook his head, knowing she wasn't going to take kindly to being told how to act.

"How dare you tell me how to conduct myself. You work for me," Margaret barked.

"No, I don't. I worked for your husband and your son, not for you," John replied pointedly.

"John, you're not helping the situation," Hans warned.

"I understand what I've told her is a shock. I can sympathize with her pain, but to take her rage out on me is misguided. I've been spending every waking hour in pursuit of whoever killed William. I only just returned and plan on heading out as soon as I get some rest," John said, defending himself.

"Hans, do you know where this ice house is?" Margaret asked, wiping the tears from her cheeks.

"Yes, I do," Hans replied.

"Take me there," she said, opening the door.

John stood and watched her leave. He thought about offering to go but knew she'd rebuff him.

Hans and Margaret left and closed the door behind them.

Exhausted, John let gravity take over. He fell onto the bed and closed his eyes. He felt for her, he truly did, and wanted to help, but what could you do when someone was acting irrationally? What he needed was rest, even a few hours. Then he'd go back out and try to find Jeremiah.

***

Panic. It was the only way to describe what Jimmy was feeling since he'd discovered Anna had been rescued. The night he returned and found the room empty and the bindings cut, he had been beset with fear that soon someone would come for him. *Who found her? Where is she? Who knows? What does it all mean?*

It wasn't enough that he hadn't been able to find Jeremiah, the one person who'd seen him and his men the morning they'd ambushed William and John; now he was plagued with thoughts of being arrested for kidnapping and rape. Yes, even in a lawless town like Deadwood, kidnapping, holding hostage and brutally raping a woman was looked down on, and the punishment for such a crime was death.

The last thing he wanted to be doing was trying to find Jeremiah when Anna was out there somewhere. His men could tell he was distant and distracted too, often commenting about how he wasn't listening or was somewhere else in thought.

Thoughts of leaving Deadwood came to him. He could do it, it made sense, but where would he go? He resisted the idea. He had built a life that would be hard to duplicate anywhere else. No, he needed to fix this, and the only way was to find the boy and Anna and kill them both.

Oliver, who had been enlisted in the hunt for Jeremiah, approached Jimmy and said, "The men are ready to go. Where to today?"

The question tore Jimmy from his troubled thoughts. "Good, good. Let me see. We'll search north of the Rothman claim and interview all the other miners we come across."

Oliver nodded and walked off.

Jimmy tossed back the remaining coffee in his cup, grabbed his belongings, and headed out but was stopped when Liam called for him.

"James, come here," Liam hollered from the second floor of the Cricket.

Jimmy sighed and turned around. "We're leaving. Don't have time."

Liam raised his brow in astonishment at Jimmy's tone. "Get your ass up here now."

"Shit," Jimmy groaned as he marched to Liam's office. He stepped inside, closed the door and asked, "Liam, you do want us to catch this kid, don't you?"

Like usual when he was stressed, Liam paced his small office. "Sit down."

"Liam, the men are waiting. We need to head out now. The marshal and his team are back. This will give us time to search without the risk of running into them."

"It's a miracle you haven't yet," Liam mused.

"It is, and I'd rather not," Jimmy said, taking a seat as Liam requested. He removed his hat and slicked his oily hair back with his free hand.

"The marshal has proven to be a pain in the ass."

"That he has. What's the point of paying people off, huh?" Jimmy rhetorically asked.

"I just received word from my man at the hotel that the widow Rothman has recently checked in. This could be a problem of the highest degree; however, this could also be an opportunity."

"You want me to—"

Liam interrupted Jimmy and said, "No, leave her be, but I need you to meet with her."

"You do?" Jimmy asked.

"Yes."

"But I need to be hunting for that boy," Jimmy said.

"And so do I, but you need to do this first," Liam said, staring down from his window onto the street below.

"Can't you do it?" Jimmy asked.

"No, I need you to. In fact, she's expecting you within the hour. Go ahead and send the others ahead to look for the boy while you meet with Mrs. Rothman."

"What am I to say to her?" Jimmy asked.

"Offer to buy the claim from her."

"Okay, so how much do you want me to buy it for?"

"Doesn't matter, but I need you to not associate me with the purchase, do you understand? You need to be buying the claim for yourself," Liam said.

"Why?"

"'Cause I said so. Now get out of my office and go meet the woman in an hour," Liam ordered.

Jimmy got to his feet and put his hat on.

"Jimmy, can I trust you?" Liam asked.

"Of course, Liam, always…um, why do you ask?"

"Do you trust me?" Liam asked.

"Yes, without question."

"Would you tell me if something was troubling you or you needed help?" Liam asked.

Concerned by the questions, Jimmy asked, "Liam, what's going on? Is there something you're not telling me?"

Liam turned and faced him. "No. I just need to hear you say it."

"Liam, you can trust me," Jimmy said.

"Growing up in Iowa, I'd often dream about the West. Life seemed dull compared to the adventures of these untamed lands. I heard stories about Lewis and Clark and their Corps of Discovery. I was enthralled; it's all I wanted to do. My best friend, Thomas Flanagan, and I pledged that when we both turned eighteen, we'd leave and follow the same route they took. Thomas was nine months older than I was. He swore he'd wait; I trusted his word. Why wouldn't I? We'd grown up together in the same dusty town. We studied the stars 'cause we knew we'd need to navigate by them later. On his eighteenth birthday, he looked me straight in the eyes and said he'd wait. The next morning I wake. I go down to get breakfast and my father tells me that he ran into Thomas' father in town and that Thomas was gone, that he left and didn't even tell his parents. He didn't leave a note, nothing. He just left and didn't look back. Now I can understand in some ways. He hated his father; that son of a bitch would beat him almost daily. What got me though was he'd looked at me the day before and told me we were best friends and that he'd wait until I turned eighteen. He lied right to my face. I look back on that. It was so easy for him. I've come to know one universal truth—all people lie, cheat, and steal. Why? 'Cause it's human. That day I told myself I'd never have an expectation that people would be honest. I find that without an expectation of honesty, I'm not shocked when someone lies or backstabs me. However, just because I don't have an expectation doesn't mean I like it."

Jimmy stood staring at Liam, unsure of what to say.

"I'll ask one more time, can I trust you?" Liam asked.

Jimmy hesitated for a second but kept with the lie. "You can trust me, Liam."

"Good, now go," Liam ordered.

Jimmy nodded and exited the office. After closing the door, his face turned ashen. *Does Liam know something about Anna?* Jimmy's stomach tightened as a nauseous sensation came over him.

"Jimmy, c'mon!" Oliver hollered from below.

"You go ahead. I'll meet you out there," Jimmy hollered and rushed to meet his men and continue the search.

***

John woke from his much-needed rest and headed straight downstairs to meet up with Con and the others to go back out in search of Jeremiah.

The early afternoons at the hotel were always quiet, and today wasn't an exception. When he cleared the last step and began to head for the entrance, he caught sight of a group of people gathered in the dining room around a table. He looked closely and noticed it was Hans, Margaret, Atkins and Jimmy. He came to a full stop, turned and marched into the dining room. "What's going on?"

Everyone at the table stopped what they were doing and looked at John.

"Mr. Nichols, good to see you," Jimmy said with a nervous smile.

Ignoring Jimmy, John pressed Hans. "What's going on?"

"Mr. O'Riodian asked for a meeting to discuss buying the claim," Hans answered.

"Mrs. Rothman, may I speak with you?" John asked.

Margaret shook her head and said, "After I'm done talking with Mr. O'Riodian."

"Ma'am, I insist," John said, a tone of urgency in his voice.

"Mr. Nichols, are you hard of hearing? I said afterwards. Now if you'll excuse us," Margaret said and went back to giving her attention to Jimmy.

"I'm sorry to be forward, but I believe the man he works for could be behind William's murder," John blurted out.

Jimmy sprang to his feet. "How dare you."

John moved his right hand to the back strap of his Colt and said, "Make your move, please."

"Mr. Nichols, I demand you leave this meeting…now!" Margaret snapped.

Hans got to his feet and stepped in between the two men. He faced John and said, "I strongly suggest you go outside and get some fresh air."

"Hans, listen to me, please."

"Where's your evidence, huh?" Jimmy barked.

"He's right, John. Where's the evidence?" Hans said.

"I, um, I'm working on that now. I just ask that while he's a suspect, you don't do business with him or his boss," John urged.

Jimmy returned John's suspicions with a half-crooked smile.

Seeing this, John pointed and snapped, "I'll prove it, I swear I will."

"I'm a businessman, Mr. Nichols, nothing more," Jimmy said. "I may work for Liam, but I'm here of my own volition. I wish to start prospecting, nothing more, and being there's no claims for sale, I thought this one might be available."

Hans pushed John back from the table and said, "Go outside, and we'll discuss this later. Right now, allow Mrs. Rothman to hear Jimmy's offer."

"Hans, he's a liar, a thief and now a murderer," John said.

"I heard that," Jimmy sneered.

John gripped his Colt firmer and glared at Jimmy.

"Go ahead, gun down an unarmed man," Jimmy said, opening his coat to show he didn't have a pistol on him.

Margaret finally stood and hollered, "Gentlemen, enough! Mr. Nichols, leave now!"

John growled under his breath and immediately exited the hotel.

Hans followed him out, grabbed him by the arm and swung him around. "Damn it, man, you need to control yourself."

"But I believe—"

"That may be fine, but she is processing everything. She has no intention of selling anything just yet."

"Don't do anything until you speak with me first," John said.

"Mrs. Rothman is a smart woman. She's merely hearing him out. She's gathering information, nothing more. She has no intention of selling anything anytime soon. After we left the ice house, she told me she wanted nothing more than to find her son's killers. She needs to collect her thoughts and go through his things. He had a journal. There may be something written in there that can shed light," Hans said.

"There was a boy who saw the men who ambushed us. All I need to do is find him. We do that, we find our killers."

"When she's done going through William's belongings, we'll all meet."

John sighed and humbly said, "I'm sorry for disturbing the meeting."

"It's fine. We're all upset over William's murder, but if we're going to find the perpetrators, we need to be smart," Hans said.

"I agree. What I need to do is link back up with the marshal and get back out."

"Yes, go find that boy," Hans said and walked back inside the hotel.

Satisfied with Hans' response, John went to get his horse at the livery and head back out in search of Jeremiah.

***

Another twelve hours of riding but no sign of Jeremiah. It was as if the boy had literally vanished. John began wondering if the boy was nothing more than a ghost. A figment of his imagination.

When nightfall came, Con called the search party off and turned everyone around.

John thought about continuing, but finding someone on a moonless night was impossible so therefore a waste of time.

With plans to ride out at dawn, John left his horse at the livery and proceeded to the hotel.

The clerk spotted John and called out, "Mr. Nichols, I have a message for you." He handed John an envelope.

"Who's this from?" John asked, seeing the envelope was blank.

"From your colleague, Mr.—"

Knowing who it was, John waved the clerk off and walked off towards his room. As he cleared the steps, he tore open the envelope and removed the letter contained. His eyes widened upon reading the contents. He immediately turned around and raced from the hotel towards his new destination...the marshal's office.

***

John burst through the door to find Hans, Margaret and Con sitting and talking. "I just got the letter."

"John, take a seat," Con said, motioning towards a lone seat next to Hans.

John nodded and greeted the others. Hans replied, but Margaret gave him a cold stare. If looks could kill, he would have been lying on the floor dead.

Con cleared his throat and adjusted himself in the creaky wooden chair. "John, Mrs. Rothman has just informed me of some interesting information. Apparently, you were to be added as a ten percent owner of the Rothman claim. Is that correct?"

Forgetting William's promise until now, John replied, "Yes."

"Would you care to elaborate why you were being given ten percent?" Con asked.

"William told me that he wanted me and Hans to have skin in the game, as he put it. He wanted partners in the enterprise, partners he could trust. He told me he wanted to gift me ten percent and, upon Hans' return, give the same to him," John carefully explained. He gave Margaret an uneasy look and asked, "How did you come by this? It was my understanding that William hadn't completed the title work."

"I found it in his journal," Margaret sneered.

"Ma'am, your tone is…I'm sorry, are you thinking I've done something wrong?"

Con shifted again in his chair, sighed and said, "Here's what I have. You say you and William were ambushed. However, the only person actually shot was Mr. Rothman and your horse. You somehow escaped without an injury—"

John cut him off and said, "Molly fell onto my leg. You want to see it? She nearly crushed it."

"John, you were the only person who saw the boy, the only other person present at the ambush. We have spent days scouring the area for Jeremiah, and we even looked diligently for any brass casings. We've found nothing. All we have are several prospectors who heard shooting, nothing else that corroborates your story. The simple facts we have are that you were slated to be a ten percent owner of a claim that was producing and suddenly the primary stakeholder is dead," Con said.

"You think I did this?"

"You're the only suspect with a motive," Margaret blurted out.

"Motive? Have I been added to the claim? Have I sought to buy you out of it?" John asked.

"It's come to our attention that you had an argument with William the other night, a heated argument," Margaret said.

"We had a disagreement, nothing more," John said defensively. "Listen, I didn't do this. I liked William. I'm telling you, the people you should be looking at intently are Liam and his man Jimmy."

"I've spoken with them. Both have alibis that have checked," Con said.

Suddenly the seriousness of the moment began to hit John. "You're serious? You think I did this."

Hans lowered his head while Margaret kept her hard stare fixed on John. Like usual, Con seemed unsure of himself but deep down was happy they had a suspect that wasn't connected to him.

"If we find Jeremiah, we will find who killed William," John stressed.

"The boy hasn't been seen for some time, and the last person to have seen him was you," Margaret said as she clenched a book in her hands. "I believe in logic, and the logic points to you. You kept my boy from coming back with his father, and now we might know why. Did you have a plan all along to kill him? Hmm? With Hans away, you had the opportunity," Margaret roared.

John took notice of the notebook and asked, "What else did William say about me?"

Margaret ignored John's question and turned to face Con. "Marshal, I expect you to do your job and arrest this man on suspicion of murdering William."

Con waved her off and replied, "Ma'am, we're merely interrogating him. At the moment we don't have any hard evidence he murdered your son. Everything is circumstantial."

"I've told you that witnesses say they argued several times about the claim, and you have my son's own words talking about gifting Mr. Nichols ten percent. He's also the only person that was there. He describes the ambush as a hail of gunfire, yet he wasn't shot, not once."

"How did you manage not to get hit?" Con asked.

"Hell if I know. Luck. I know my horse Molly was struck," John replied. He began to think of running. If they were seeking justice at any costs, he didn't want to be the collateral damage to finding it.

Hans remained unusually quiet, instead fiddling with the button on his overcoat.

"Defend me, damn it," John snapped at Hans. "This morning we were going to work together to find the killers, now this?"

"I'm sorry, my friend, I can't. To be honest, I hardly know ya. And we went and did our own investigation. So many told of you being heated against William, you openly challenging him," Hans answered.

"I'm telling you, Liam did this. He wants that claim back," John said.

"It's natural for someone to see an opportunity and go for it. Jimmy is a businessman, like Liam," Con said, defending Jimmy and Liam as he leaned on his desk and folded his hands. He was settling into the idea that John would be the prime suspect and now needed one last thing to seal his fate and have him arrested.

"Are we done here?" John asked, looking around the room.

"Do you want to make a statement of guilt? If you do, we'd petition for mercy," Con said.

"The only statement I'm making is I'm innocent," he said, standing. "Unless you're going to arrest me, I'm going to go back out and search for Jeremiah."

"Marshal, you can't let him leave," Margaret beseeched.

Con stood and approached John. "She's right, Mr. Nichols. You're under arrest for the murder of William Rothman."

"This is bullshit," John said, stepping back and putting his hand on his Colt.

"Don't, John, please don't," Hans urged.

"You pull that gun, I'll kill ya. You hear me?" Con roared, holding his hand near his pistol.

"I didn't do this," John said. "Hans, please believe me. I need you to go find Jeremiah. He'll tell you who did this, please."

"I'll continue to search, but in the meantime, I need you to surrender to the marshal," Hans said, standing and approaching John with his hands out in front of him.

"Swear to me," John said.

"I swear on my honor as a soldier," Hans replied.

John looked deeply into Hans' eyes and found him to be honest. He raised his arms above his head and turned around. "I surrender, but under protest, for I am innocent."

CHAPTER ELEVEN

"At his best, man is the noblest of all animals; separated from law and justice he is the worst." – Aristotle

DEADWOOD, DAKOTA TERRITORY

OCTOBER 21, 1876

Word of John's arrest spread through the town like wildfire, with many assuming he was guilty.

When news reached Liam and Jimmy, they both rejoiced. One reason was they didn't have to spend a penny in order to secure this breach of justice, and second, for the peace of mind that they'd committed the crime and another man would pay the price. There was one thread left hanging, and that was Jeremiah, but no one had seen or heard of the boy since before the ambush.

Although Liam felt like a weight had been lifted, he wouldn't rest until the boy was found. Each day and night, he sent Jimmy and a team out to scour the countryside, but every time they came back empty-handed.

Jimmy rode in, his legs and buttocks throbbing from a long ride. He dismounted his horse and handed the reins to a new doorman recently hired for the Cricket. "Take it to the livery," he ordered.

The man took the horse without question and

marched off.

Jimmy entered the bar to find Liam in his usual morning spot.

Liam looked up from his paper and hollered, "Well, look what the cat dragged in. Any luck, James?"

"Same," Jimmy said, sauntering up to the bar.

"Coffee?" Liam asked, placing an empty cup in front of Jimmy.

"That and a beer," Jimmy said, leaning his full weight against the bar. He removed his hat and set it next to him. "Liam, I think the boy is gone. I think he got the life scared out of him and took off. I don't think we'll see him again."

Liam poured a coffee and placed a glass of beer next to it. "That may be the case, but we need to keep looking in the meantime. The trial is in two days. We can't have that boy show and foul everything up."

"I agree, but looking for that son of a whore is wearing us all out. Thankfully, I have us split into two twelve-hour shifts, but it's definitely putting a lot of stress on us," Jimmy complained.

"I heard that German bastard is also out there looking. It appears Mr. Nichols still has a friend willing to help him out. We can't afford to have him find the boy."

"You don't think I know that," Jimmy grumbled.

"Your attitude isn't appreciated, but I'll chalk it up to fatigue. Take your drinks, head upstairs and take a bath. Grab a piece of pussy too," Liam offered.

The bar doors swung open and a shadowy figure entered. He removed his black bowler hat and made his way to the bar.

"If it isn't the Pinkerton detective," Liam said when he recognized it was Garrett.

"Mr. Prince, good to see you, and it's Jimmy, right?" Garrett said, nodding to both.

"I heard you were leaving, had a new assignment. What brings you into my fine establishment?" Liam asked.

Garrett stopped short of the bar, smoothed out his thin mustache with his left hand, and replied, "I do have a new assignment, and it happens to be here in Deadwood."

Jimmy could hear the call of the hot bath, but his curiosity to know what Garrett was still doing in Deadwood kept him glued to his spot.

"You don't say. Are you allowed to share this new assignment?"

"I came here to specifically to speak with you about my new case," Garrett said, removing a small notebook from his coat pocket. He opened it, removed a small pencil, turned to a blank page and asked, "On the morning William Rothman was murdered, where were you, Liam?"

Taken aback by the question, Liam struck out with his own question. "What is this?"

"A simple question," Garrett answered, his expression stoic.

"The murderer has been arrested already. The trial is in two days," Liam said, flummoxed. "I suggest you go speak with the marshal before you come in here asking questions and wasting everyone's time."

"Were you here?" Garrett asked Liam, ignoring his statement.

Jimmy rose and stood erect. He turned to Garrett and asked, "Who hired you?"

"I work for Mr. Nichols. Now can you please answer the question, Mr. Prince?" Garrett asked.

***

If Garrett Vane was anything, he was determined. He was originally sent to Deadwood to find the son of a sitting United States senator, and although the case seemed impossible to solve, he'd found out exactly what had happened.

After a night of gambling, the senator's son left a small gambling tent near the edge of town. He was loaded down with winnings and drunk. Maybe it was the alcohol or the lack of life experience; but whatever it was, he walked out of that tent without a concern or thought that he had just won enough coin and gold to equal a man's yearly wage. As he stumbled back to the hovel he was living in, he sang and boasted to anyone who'd hear about how much he'd just made at the poker table. His siren song hit the ears of the wrong people, and within minutes, he was lying in an alleyway, his head split open and his winnings stolen. In order to cover their crime, the two men, who were unsuccessful prospectors, took the body just outside town and buried it. Garrett was finally able to find the men responsible when a last-ditch effort was approved to post a reward for any information that led to the whereabouts of the senator's son. It took only a few hours of the posting for one of the men responsible to come forward and claim he'd seen something, and he led Garrett to the shallow grave. Of course, Garrett was suspect of the man's eyewitness claim, and after spending half a day interrogating him, the man broke and told the truth. By the end of the day, both men were turned over to Marshal Stapleton, and the senator's son's body was transported to Yankton in order to be put on a train to Washington, DC.

Upon completing his case, Garrett was preparing to leave when word came that John Nichols had been arrested, and shortly after he received a personal message from John requesting he help investigate his case and find the real killers of William. While Garrett liked John, he took the case only after approval from the Chicago office and after receiving a retainer payment of three thousand dollars.

Garrett believed John was innocent, but finding the true killers would take the same level of determination he had in solving the senator's son's case along with some incentives and a level of creativity to go along with it.

***

Liam lived in the back of the Cricket but had a safe house in town he used for special occasions, and housing Anna was one of those.

Liam entered the house to find Doc Hardy packing

up his bag. "How is she?"

"Better and better each day. I'd say she'll be able to get back to whatever she wants to soon," Hardy replied, looking curiously at the bouquet of flowers clutched in Liam's left hand.

"What's soon?" Liam asked, looking past Hardy and into the bedroom, where Anna lay staring out the window.

"Two days, maybe three," Hardy answered. "Say, Liam, I know you told me not to ask, but does she have a home?"

Liam cocked his head and sighed.

"No questions, right," Hardy said, walking past Liam towards the front door. "I'll return tomorrow and check in on her." Hardy exited the house, closing the door behind him.

With only Liam and Anna in the house, Liam headed into the bedroom and asked, "How are you feeling today?"

"Good," she answered without giving Liam a glance.

"I brought these for you," Liam said, holding the flowers up.

Anna looked at them; a slight smile graced her face, which showed signs of improvement. "They're nice."

"I'll put them over here," Liam said, placing them on the nightstand. He wiped his hands nervously on his trousers and grabbed a chair. He placed it next to the bed and sat down. "Doc says you'll be well enough to leave in a couple of days. Like I promised, I'll let you go with cash in hand but not before you do me that favor."

"Will you?" she asked, a tone of disbelief in her voice.

"Of course, yes. I just need you to do one small thing for me. Then when you're done, you can go anywhere you want," Liam said.

"What do you need me to do?" she asked.

"There's a man who's been arrested for murder. I need you to testify that he also killed your husband and kidnapped you," Liam said slowly, making sure to emphasize each word so she understood.

Anna looked at him, confused, and said, "Jimmy is in jail?"

"No, this man is named John Nichols. He's been arrested for the murder of another man. I need to make sure he is also tried for your husband's murder and your kidnapping," Liam clarified.

"But Jimmy murdered my husband; he told me. He was the one who also kidnapped and raped me, not this John Nichols. No, I can't bear false testimony against this other man," Anna said defiantly.

"This is the favor I need. Once you do that, you can go. Now think about it for a couple of days. The trial is in two days," Liam said and stood up.

"I don't think I can," she said.

He patted her hand and said, "Just think about it. I'll be back tomorrow to check on you. If you need anything, I have a man stationed just outside." He exited the dimly lit room and stepped into the front room. He turned back and said, "Remember, once you do this for me, you're free to go."

"Then I'm your prisoner too?" she shot back.

"Not at all, we made a deal. I expect you to live up to your side of it, nothing more," Liam said.

***

Garret arrived at the marshal's office so he could speak with John. Con let him past and went back to reading the *Irish Times* newspaper he received monthly.

In the back of the marshal's office were two jail cells. John was housed in one, and the two men arrested for the senator's son's murder were in the other.

Garrett got close to the iron bars of John's cell and called him over. "John, wake up."

Unable to sleep deeply, John heard Garrett, opened his eyes and sat up quickly. "Any news?"

"I've conducted a lot of interviews. Nothing new to add. We need to find that boy. He's the one saving grace unless we get someone to turn in Liam or Jimmy."

"Is Hans still looking for him?" John asked.

"Yes, he is," Garrett said. "Listen, I suggest you hire an attorney too. I don't think it's a good idea to represent yourself."

"Look who it is!" a voice growled from the other cell.

John looked past Garrett to see one of the men leering at them. "How about minding your own business."

"Don't be fooled. That Pinkerton is a low-down liar. He tricked us," the man spewed.

Garrett chuckled at the man's response.

"Liar? From what I hear, you're just a damn idiot," John snapped back at the man.

"To hell with you," the man said.

"Pay no mind to them," Garrett said.

"Where were we?" John asked.

"Lawyer, you need one, and in the meantime, I'll keep asking around, see if I can find someone willing to give up some vital information," Garrett said.

John leaned in and said, "Be careful what you say around the marshal. I don't trust him."

"Don't worry, I'm not telling anyone anything, not even Hans."

"Have you had a chance to speak with Mrs. Rothman?" John asked.

"I tried. She won't see me."

"Why is she so sure I've done this? I don't understand. Did William write something disparaging about me? She's determined to see me tried and hanged for this."

"I can't say why, but that woman has her eyes set on you, that's for sure," Garrett confirmed.

John couldn't understand why Margaret was so adamant that he had killed William. Why would she not take the time to ensure she had the right person? This was one of the biggest questions he tortured himself with as he lay in his cell. "Will Hans speak with you?"

"Yes, but I'm careful, like I said, on what I tell him. I only give him information that I feel is needed and nothing more unless I want to feed him some disinformation to…wait a minute, hold on. I've got a way…I think I may have come up with a way to flush out the real killers," Garrett said excitedly.

"Tell me," John urged.

Garrett looked back and saw the man still staring and in earshot. "No, not here. Let me run with this and see what comes up." Garrett stood and went to leave.

John reached through the bars and grabbed him. "I've only got two days, less even. Hurry, please."

"If my plan works, you'll be out of here soon enough," Garrett replied and quickly rushed off.

***

When the door opened, John expected to see Con or Garrett standing in the open doorway, not Margaret.

She strode inside with Con right behind her with a stool.

"Here ma'am," Con said placing the stool in front of John's cell.

John sat up and watched her carefully wondering what she wanted.

Margaret took a seat and turned to Con, "If you don't mind."

"Of course," Con said exiting the area, closing the door behind him.

A warm light came in from the backdoor window. The golden beams hit her diamond earrings causing them to glitter.

The two men in the adjacent cell were both fast

asleep, their guttural snores made Margaret cringe.

"What do you want?" John asked, not feigning politeness.

"You be quiet, I'm here to talk, not you," Margaret fired back.

"You may talk but who says I'll listen?" John asked leaning back against the cold wall.

"When my son told me he wanted to come west, I thought he was merely talking. You know boys, they have these dreams of adventure. I think it comes from their fathers and the books they read. Nevertheless, I didn't pay much attention to William as he often talked about doing overtly masculine things but never did. I foolishly thought this talk of going west to mine for gold as one of those, I clearly was wrong. When I saw William was serious as was Horatio I should have stood my ground more but I didn't. I listened to Horatio, he thought William needed a little seasoning and being the dutiful wife, I finally gave in." She paused and removed a handkerchief from her clutch purse. She dabbed her eyes and continued. "William was meant to take over for Horatio at the bank but that will never happen because of you, Mister Nichols."

"Me? I didn't do anything but my job," John said defensively.

"If your job was to inspire my son, you were successful, if it was to protect him; you failed miserably," Margaret seethed.

"You son was stronger than you give him credit for. I attempted to talk him out of getting that claim until we could find out more about it. I told him numerous times that dealing with Liam was a mistake."

"You failed my son, there's nothing more to say. I hold you one hundred percent responsible. If you hadn't been, you, he'd still be here. It pains me to say, but he looked up to you; he wrote as much, but know that won't make it into evidence tomorrow. What will is that you several times intimidated him so much he wrote that he could imagine you killing him. What upsets me the most was he found that alluring and wanted to be like you. He wanted to be feared."

"He wanted to be respected, that's what he wanted," John blurted out interrupting her.

"Mister Nichols, you will soon be tried and I'm quite confident convicted. You alone are the one responsible for William's murder."

"I've done nothing wrong and I most assuredly didn't murder William. I counted him a friend," John snapped.

"Don't use that word, a friend would have insisted he come back home to bury his father."

"I did but he didn't want to hear any of it," John said.

She clenched her jaw and wringed her hands tightly together. "I'm done here. Mister Nichols, may you rot in hell." She stood and went to the door. "Marshal, I'm done here."

The door creaked open and Margaret stepped through it.

"The real killers are still out there, you're making a

mistake. Don't let his death go without justice!" John hollered after her.

CHAPTER TWELVE

"All warfare is deception." – Unknown

DEADWOOD, DAKOTA TERRITORY

OCTOBER 23, 1876

When John entered the McDaniel Theater, he was shocked by the number of people assembled. The spectators counted in the dozens. He was escorted past them to a small table on the left and was ordered to sit. He scanned the room for Garrett, but he was nowhere to be found. To his right stood another table. Seated there was Samuel Atkins; he had been hired to prosecute the case for Deadwood. In front of John sat Rufus Pendleton, he was a judge brought in from Yankton. In the far corner sat a dozen men—some miners, others were local businessmen—all assembled to be jurors.

Trials weren't held often in Deadwood, but when they were, the cost was financed by a joint venture between the businesses or sometimes by a single individual. Today's trial was being paid for by Margaret.

The theater was loud and lively, with many discussing the pending case and money being wagered in the back on the outcome.

Rufus slammed a mallet down and shouted, "Let's bring the court to order!"

People still talked loudly.

Rufus banged the mallet several more times against the table and hollered, "Court is in session. Everyone shut up!"

The theater grew quiet.

"Today we are here for the trial of John Nichols, who has been indicted for the murder of William Rothman. We shall proceed with opening statements, first from the prosecution, then the defense. The camp is being represented by Samuel Atkins and the defense by…Mr. Nichols, where is your counselor?"

John stood and replied, "I'm representing myself, Your Honor."

"Are you sure that's what you want to do?" Rufus asked.

"Yes, Your Honor," John answered.

"Very well, take a seat and we shall proceed," Rufus said.

Atkins stood and stated the case against John. His basis for convicting him stood on three circumstantial items: one, John was the only person with William at the time of the ambush; two, he was to receive an ownership stake in the claim; and finally, the supposed numerous derogatory character references mentioned by William in his journal. When Atkins finished, he sat down and turned to face John.

"Mr. Nichols, your turn," Rufus said.

John had lain in his cell and thought about what he'd say. He just hoped it sounded better spoken versus in his head. He rose, turned toward the jury and said, "I am innocent of the murder of William. In fact, I am also a victim of that horrible crime. While I wasn't struck by a round, my horse, Molly, was killed. I nearly suffered a crushed leg and lost a new friend. You see, William and I had grown to like and respect each other in the days since we left Dodge City. I got to see how hard he worked and how determined he was to make his parents proud. After his father died, William could have left and gone; but he didn't, he chose to stay and continue to work the claim. He showed—"

"Liar!" Margaret hollered.

Everyone turned towards Margaret. The courtroom burst into gasps and loud chatter.

"Order in the court!" Rufus hollered, banging his mallet numerous times until the room fell quiet. "The defendant can continue."

"I'll finish by saying this. I did not do what I'm accused of. They don't have any evidence to the fact I did it. They claim there are passages in his journal that implicate me, and I look forward to hearing what those are so I can debunk them," John said and sat down.

Rufus faced Atkins and said, "Present your first witness."

One after another Atkins had people come forward. Most John didn't know. All were asked the one question that was fast becoming the main evidence against John. *'Did you ever hear Mr. Rothman state something to the effect that John might want to kill him?'* All would answer yes, and when it came time to cross-examine, John was at a loss, so he'd just pass. The one witness whose words hurt the most was Margaret. She read several passages from

William's journal, and in them he stated something similar to what he'd said during the two heated discussions, and that was John would give him looks that seemed intimidating and threatening. And she quoted him by reading one passage specifically, *John is a hard man, a killer for sure. This is why my father and I hired him. He's quick with his draw and lethal. I just hope he doesn't turn those skills against me one day. But I'll be the first to admit that the looks he gives me sometimes are terrifying. I'm not sure if he'll turn on me or not.'* Slowly but surely it was looking as if John's demise was certain, without the most damaging witness yet to come, Anna.

"Your Honor, I need to call a witness that I haven't listed yet. May I do so?" Atkins asked Rufus.

"Who is this witness?" Rufus asked. "Actually, come here. Let's discuss this quietly."

Atkins and John both came to Rufus.

"Who is this witness?" Rufus asked quietly so no one could overhear.

"She's a victim and eyewitness to another murder, her husband, a murder Mr. Nichols is suspected of committing."

"What? I don't know what you're talking about," John protested.

"She will give testimony that will bolster the case that Mr. Nichols is a murderer," Atkins said.

"Your Honor, I haven't killed anyone, and I don't know anything about a woman whose husband I killed," John said, raising his voice louder than he should have.

The two men began to squabble.

Rufus pounded his mallet and said, "Silence."

Both men adhered to his call and stood quietly.

"This is peculiar, counselor. If Mr. Nichols is being accused of another murder, why hasn't this woman come forward until now?"

"I only just found out, Your Honor," Atkins replied.

Rufus rubbed his chin and thought. "I won't allow it. If this woman has a complaint, she needs to notify the marshal. Otherwise it has no pertinence on this particular case."

"But, Your Honor," Atkins protested.

"That's my final decision."

Both men returned to their seats. John got a victory albeit a small one.

Atkins shook his head at Liam, who was standing in the far corner.

"If the prosecution is finished, the defense will now present witnesses," Rufus said, looking at John.

John didn't have a strong defense, and he didn't have any witnesses. Hans had warned him not to call him, and without him, he had no one. "Your Honor—"

From the back of the room, Garrett cried out, "We found him, the boy, we found him!"

All eyes turned on Garrett as he pushed his way through to John's side.

"You found him?" John asked.

Garrett leaned in and whispered, "Play along."

Loud chatter erupted across the room.

Rufus began to pound his mallet, but it was unsuccessful as the volume rose in the theater. Everyone knew what finding Jeremiah meant. If the boy had seen who had committed the ambush, then the entire outcome of the trial was in doubt.

"Order in the courtroom!" Rufus hollered, but no one paid him any attention.

Garrett stood and called out, "We found him. He's being brought here now, on the eastern road."

"Sir, who are you?" Rufus asked.

"I'm Garret Vane, with the Pinkerton Detective Agency. I've been hired by Mr. Nichols," Garrett answered.

The theater turned into panic as people were pointing fingers and talking loudly.

Unable to bring the room under control, Rufus hollered, "The court is adjourned until tomorrow morning." He slammed down the mallet and exited the theater through the back exit.

"I'm going to get off. I can't believe it," John said, noticeably happy.

"Not quite yet," Garrett said. He pulled John close and whispered, "I don't have him. This is all a trap. Let's see if the rats start to jump from the sinking ship."

"You don't have him?" John asked.

"No, I hired a boy to masquerade as him and got Phillip Barns to help out. He's transporting the boy here from your claim."

"Barns is helping?" John asked.

"You have more friends than you know, and people are also tired of certain folks literally getting away with murder. I even have the Earp brothers helping," Garrett replied.

"You're baiting the killers; that's dangerous and risky. Why have him ride out to the claim and come back?" John asked.

"It's all about appearances. And as you said, it is dangerous, but this is a good way to lure the killers out into the open," Garrett said. He looked and found Liam talking aggressively to Jimmy. "If I'm correct, we'll soon find out who really did it, as people have a knack for self-preservation."

Knowing what it all meant, Liam rushed to Jimmy, who was close by in the room. "That damn boy will end us all."

"I'll...um, I'll go find them and stop them," Jimmy said, panicked.

"You're going to kill everyone?" Liam asked, gripping Jimmy's arm tightly.

"What choice do we have?" Jimmy asked.

Hearing that, Liam shoved Jimmy out of the way and raced off through the crowd, pushing people out of the way.

Watching Liam leave in a hurry, Garrett stood and said, "It appears we already have a bite."

TWO MILES EAST OF DEADWOOD, DAKOTA TERRITORY

Unsure of where Liam had gone, Jimmy took it upon himself to go find the boy and kill him. It had to be done and quickly. He took a horse from the livery and rode out along the eastern road.

His heart was racing so much his chest hurt. He'd been through much, but this was more than he'd had to deal with before. Seeing Liam in a panic caused him to be as well. It was his mistake and his to clean up.

He cleared a corner in the road and ran into Phillip Barns behind the reins of a wagon. He pulled hard on the horse and stopped in front of him.

Phillip brought the wagon to a stop and said, "Jimmy, you're in my way."

"Phillip, I hear you've got the wildling boy. Is that true?" Jimmy asked.

"I don't believe that's any of your business. Now if you can get out of my way, I need to get to town."

Jimmy reached back for his pistol, but Phillip drew first.

"I don't want to shoot you, but I will. Now turn around and ride off. There's nothing in this wagon for you," Phillip said, holding his pistol steady, the muzzle pointing directly at Jimmy's chest.

"You're making a mistake," Jimmy barked.

Two others rode up behind Jimmy. He turned and saw it was Wyatt and Morgan Earp. "Barns, I hear you might be in need of an armed escort," Wyatt said, giving Jimmy a hard stare.

"That would be nice," Phillip said, holstering his Colt.

"You're all making a huge mistake. Do you know who you're siding against?" Jimmy asked, his face flush and eyes wide.

"You best head on back into town and tell your puppet master the boy is coming into town and will be seeing the judge first."

Jimmy pulled his horse around and bolted back to town.

DEADWOOD, DAKOTA TERRITORY

Jimmy jumped from his horse and didn't bother to tie him up; instead he ran into the Cricket. "Liam, where are you?" All eyes turned and watched as he frantically shoved his way through the bar patrons, up the stairs and into Liam's office. "Liam, the boy—" he said but stopped talking when he saw who was gathered around Liam's desk.

Atkins, Con and Anna turned and stared at Jimmy, who stood in the open doorway.

"James, good timing. Please come in," Liam said, pointing towards a fourth chair in the corner. "You're just the person we wanted to see."

"Anna?" Jimmy said, dumbfounded. She was the last person he expected to see.

She scowled at him but didn't say a word.

"Liam, what's going on?"

"Close the door and you'll find out," Liam replied.

"I need to talk to you in private...now," Jimmy said, his voice cracking under the pressure.

"Sit...down...now!" Liam barked.

Jimmy closed the door and went to the vacant seat.

"James, I've spoken with Atkins. He will do his best

for you, and Con here says he will talk with the judge about leniency after the conviction. We think we can get him to give you life in prison back in Yankton," Liam said.

"Huh?" Jimmy asked. "I'm not going down for this, no, never. It wasn't my idea. Nope, not going to happen. Marshal, listen to me, killing Rothman wasn't my idea, it was Liam's," Jimmy blurted out and pointed at Liam.

Acting shocked, Liam leaned back in his chair, the wood creaking as he placed his full weight into it. "I'm sorry to hear you say that, after all that I've done for you and after what I've done for you here. I'm helping you. When I found this young girl, she told me a tale of horror. At first I was confused that it was Mr. Nichols, but she claimed it was the man who killed Rothman, but now we know that was you. As you can see, there was a misunderstanding. Her English isn't very good, but she's now made a statement, and the marshal has accepted it. Everything you're saying now is just in bad taste."

Jimmy shot to his feet and pulled his pistol. He held it up with a shaking hand and hollered, "I'm not going to let you use me as a scapegoat!"

Con, known as a quick draw, pulled his Colt, aimed, and didn't hesitate. He pulled the trigger and struck Jimmy squarely in the chest.

Jimmy clutched the wound and fell backwards, dropping his pistol.

Anna watched with glee. A smile stretched across her face as the man who had tortured her was dying slowly.

Liam sprang to his feet, as did Atkins. Liam to see

what had happened and Atkins out of fear.

"I trusted you," Jimmy said to Liam.

"And I you, so sorry to see you weren't worthy of my trust," Liam said, feigning concern.

Jimmy's hand crawled its way towards his pistol.

Seeing this, Con cocked his pistol and fired once more, this time hitting Jimmy in the forehead.

"Why did you do that?" Liam asked.

"He was going for his pistol. Can't take any chances," Con replied, holstering his gun.

"Well, Marshal, we've found our killer. I expect you'll be briefing the judge on the matter?" Liam asked.

"I will. Thank you for your time, Liam," Con said and promptly left.

Atkins stood staring at the widening pool of blood.

"Counselor, come see me tomorrow. I'll have the retainer fee I promised for James," Liam said, winking at Atkins.

"Sounds good, Liam." Atkins nodded and raced out of the room.

Liam turned and knelt next to his safe, entered the code and opened it. He pulled out a bag of coins and a stack of cash. He set it on the desk in front of Anna and said, "As promised."

Anna looked at the money. It was more than she'd ever seen at one time. She was anxious to leave, but before she could go, she had one last thing to do. She got up and walked over to Jimmy's body, yelled something in Swedish, then spit on him.

Liam simply smiled.

She returned, grabbed the bag and cash, and asked, "Wagon and horse?"

"Go see Steffen at the livery. He'll have it ready for you," Liam asked.

"To hell with this place," she snapped and marched off.

Liam put his gaze back on Jimmy's body and said, "What a damn mess." He shook his head and sighed. "Oliver, Oliver!"

The ever-obedient Oliver appeared almost instantly. "Yes, boss."

"Clean up this mess, but don't take his body to the hogs. Have him delivered to the undertaker."

"Yes, boss," Oliver said and turned to leave.

"Oh, Oliver," Liam said.

Oliver stopped and said, "Yes."

"Do you trust me?" Liam asked.

Finding the question odd, but knowing he needed to answer, he replied, "Yes."

"Can I trust you?" Liam asked.

"Absolutely," Oliver answered, his spine stiffening as he almost came to attention like a faithful soldier.

"Good, I'm going to be needing a new right-hand man. You up for the task?" Liam asked.

"Why, Liam, um, that's unexpected."

"Well?"

"It would be an honor. You can trust me to do anything. I won't let you down. I'll do anything you ask," Oliver said, beaming with excitement.

"Anything?"

"Yes, boss, anything."

"Good, come in and close the door."

Oliver did as he said and stood patiently waiting to hear his first official duty as Liam's right-hand man.

"That square head woman who just left, she has something of mine, and I want it back. Can you take care of her…discreetly?"

Oliver nodded and said, "Whatever you say, Liam."

CHAPTER THIRTEEN

"A hero cannot be a hero unless in a heroic world." –
Nathaniel Hawthorne

DEADWOOD, DAKOTA TERRITORY

OCTOBER 27, 1876

As fast as the word had spread that he'd been arrested, so did the word that Jimmy had been the real killer behind William's death and had paid the ultimate price. For John, all he could do was be thankful he'd hired Garrett because without him, he would have been hanged.

The day after word broke about Jimmy, John tried to reconcile with Margaret, but she wanted nothing to do with him, no doubt still blaming him for William's demise. Hans had confided that he'd misspoken in New York and made it sound like John was responsible for William staying in Deadwood. There was nothing John could say or do. She was hurting, and all John represented was William's betrayal and ultimate death.

Escorted by Hans, Margaret departed Deadwood on October 26 but not before she had sold the claim to Liam. What no one knew was everything had come full circle, Liam had originally sold the claim to Sven, then to William, and now had it back again.

Upon hearing about the sale, John decided he was done with Deadwood. Like John, Morgan Earp had had enough of Deadwood and invited John to come back to Dodge City, but he declined. However, his brother Wyatt wished to stay. An opportunity to haul lumber presented itself, and being that Wyatt was ever the entrepreneur, he jumped at it. The opportunity would span the winter months, and Wyatt needed help, so naturally Wyatt offered him a position. John couldn't imagine what Deadwood was like during the harsh winter months, and there wasn't any desire to find out.

Once more John found himself pondering his next move. He'd wandered and zigzagged his way across the United States since leaving Georgia back in 1865, and now needed another place to go; but where?

He thought of going back to Arizona Territory and California came to mind; then again there was promise to be had in western Washington too. All his interests seemed to point west, not one thing called him to travel east; at least none had presented itself.

When he found himself lost, he often found wisdom in a bottle, and the best place to get a drink was the Number Ten Saloon.

He pushed the door open and found it as busy as usual. He made his way to the bar, found a spot and squeezed in.

The bartender recognized him and without asking brought over a bottle and a single glass. "On the house."

"For what?" John asked.

"For helping Jimmy O'Riodian get what was coming to him. I hated the greasy son of a bitch," the old bartender said. He spit out a wad of tobacco juice, wiped his lower lip and chuckled. "Oh, what I would've given to see that devilish bastard get shot."

John pulled the cork on the bottle and poured his glass full. "I'm sure it was a sight to see."

"Well, good for ya. Glad it was him and not you," the old man said, then retreated to the far side of the bar.

"There you are," Garrett said, walking up behind John.

John swung around and replied, "I thought you had left."

"I was scheduled to, but I got a telegram," Garrett answered, holding up a piece of paper.

"New assignment?" John asked.

"As a matter of fact, it is," Garrett replied, leaning up against the bar. He waved to the bartender, who brought over a glass.

"Anywhere exciting?" John asked.

"Missouri, St. Joseph area, north of Kansas City," Garrett answered.

"Nice town, spent a little time there years back," John said.

"Visiting or business?"

Thoughts came of his last time there and the man he'd killed in Westport.

"You seem lost in thought," Garrett said.

"Oh, it's nothing. Just thinking about the last time I was in Kansas City," John replied before downing his entire glass of whiskey.

"She must have been gorgeous," Garrett joked, elbowing John in the arm.

"Seems like a lifetime ago. So tell me, what's in Kansas City?" John asked.

"St. Joseph."

"Right, St. Joseph. Is it a princess or rich tycoon needing you to solve a robbery?"

"Something better," Garrett replied with a gleaming smile.

John gave him a surprised look and asked, "Do tell."

"Ever heard of the James and Younger Gang?"

"Yeah, I heard they got shot up in Minnesota this past summer," John replied.

"They did, most of the Youngers were captured, but the James brothers escaped. Rumor is they're back in Missouri, possibly near St. Joe. The Adams Express Company still would like to see them brought to justice. So they've rehired us to go try."

"Wait a minute. Didn't I read somewhere you tried to get them before? It was in…"

"Back in '75, but it didn't work out. Our founder has made this personal, wants to try again. It's not an easy operation. We've lost others trying to infiltrate. The James brothers are considered Robin Hoods of sorts to the locals, Goddamn folk heroes. We can't get a peep out of any of them. Being that I'm a Southerner and former confederate veteran, I've been tasked with trying to go deep undercover."

"You like risky endeavors, don't you?" John asked.

"Here's the catch. I need a partner, but Chicago doesn't hire many sons of the South, so I thought of you," Garrett said, his eyes wide with anticipation of what

John would say. "The boss thinks if we're former Confederates they might take kindly to us, make it easier to get in."

John straightened his posture, furrowed his brow and asked, "You want me to work for the Pinkerton Detective Agency?"

"Yes."

"And try to infiltrate the James and Younger Gang?"

"What's left of it, meaning just the James brothers—Jesse and Frank."

John's head spun with conflicting responses. The job sounded exciting but also highly dangerous. The James and Younger Gang were notorious and ruthless. The man who they believed informed on them was found dead and two Pinkerton's were gunned down back in 1875 so the job was more than not easy, it was highly dangerous and could almost be considered a suicide mission. "Listen, I don't know."

"You're perfect. You're from Georgia, a veteran, you can talk the talk; plus I need help. The pay is great, fifty dollars per week."

"Fifty a week? Why so much?"

"Hazardous duty pay," Garrett answered. "So what do you say?"

"You sure they're in Missouri?" John asked.

"We're not sure, but if our intelligence leads us elsewhere, we'll go there," Garrett answered.

The more he thought about the opportunity, the more it sounded like it was made for him. He turned to Garrett and asked, "When do we leave for Missouri?"

THREE MILES EAST OF DEADWOOD

John and Garret rode in silence, neither had much to say. All John could do was think about his time in Deadwood. If he were to be asked to describe it in one word, he'd say, deadly. And deadly is what it was. He'd come to town with three other men, two of them were now gone. One from disease and one from the hand of another man. If he were asked if he'd do all over again, he'd answer, no.

Garret pulled the reins on his horse and said, "I've gotta take a leak."

"Okay," John said slowing his horse until he came to a full stop.

Garret dismounted and walked to the side of the trail. He whistled as he went.

John kept his focus on the road ahead and the surrounding area, the last thing he needed was to walk into another ambush.

Garret stopped whistling suddenly and called out, "Hey John, um, come here."

"What is it?" John asked spinning around in the saddle.

"We're being watched," Garret said slowly buttoning up his trousers.

John ripped the Colt from his holster and held it out in front of him.

"I don't think you'll need that," Garret said.

"Huh?" John queried, curious as to what he could be talking about.

"That boy you were looking for, I think he's right over there," Garret said pointing towards a large bush.

John quickly dismounted and walked over to where Garret was standing. He looked and instantly spotted

Jeremiah's dirty but youthful face staring back. "Well what do you know."

Garret raised his hand and waved.

"I've got an idea," John said and raced back to his saddle bag. He opened it and pulled out some hard tack. He came back, held it up and said, "Food."

Jeremiah nodded.

John placed it on the ground and said, "Back away, he needs some space."

Garret did as he said. The two stepped back some thirty feet and waited.

Minutes later Jeremiah appeared on the edge of the trail, snatched the pieces of hard tack and dashed off for the security of the bush.

John came forward and asked, "It's good to see you. I'm glad you're alive."

Jeremiah looked up but didn't respond, his focus was on devouring the hard tack.

"That kid is the hands down winner of hide and seek," Garret joked.

"Yep."

"How ironic, when you don't need him he appears. This kid caused you some stress," Gareet said.

"Not at all, this kid saved my life, what happened afterwards was what it was. The boy must have known people were searching for him and had the instincts to know that some of those people wanted him dead."

"I guess that's one way of looking at it," Garret said.

"More?" John asked.

Jeremiah nodded.

John got a few more pieces, set them on the ground and said, "Goodbye, Jeremiah."

Jeremiah stopped chewing, wiped his mouth and replied, "Goodbye."

A slight smile stretched across John's face. He mounted his horse, turned towards Garret and said, "C'mon, we've got a train to catch."

EPILOGUE

"The people of western Missouri are, in some respects, very peculiar. We will take Jackson county where I was born for instance. In that section the people seemed to be born fighters, the instinct being inherited from a long line of ancestors." – Cole Younger

ST. JOSEPH, MISSOURI

NOVEMBER 3, 1876

John stepped off the train. He looked around the small depot and instantly felt a familiarity with the place. He couldn't quite peg it, but something felt…right.

A conductor strutted by in a hurry.

"Excuse me," John said, calling after the conductor.

The man stopped. He gave John an irritated look. "Yes."

"Where can I find—"

"John Nance? Are you John Nance?" a man asked from across the depot.

John looked and saw an elderly man waving.

Seeing John was distracted, the conductor rushed off.

"Yes, I'm John Nance. Are you Daniel Askew?"

"That's me. Now come on, we have an hour's ride back to the farm," Daniel said. He was an older man, sixty-seven to be exact, with white wispy hair, deep-set wrinkles, and deep blue eyes.

John followed him to a wagon, tossed his bag in the back and climbed on.

Daniel took a bit longer to climb on board due to his age and condition. He whipped the single horse, and the wagon lurched forward.

An awkward silence fell over the two for the first thirty minutes. John hated just sitting there quietly, so he decided to start a conversation. "How long you been growing tobacco?"

"The farm has been growing tobacky since my daddy was a little un."

"So why the advertisement for help? Seems you could find some able-bodied men around here to help," John asked.

"Nope, the damn war killed most young folk, and any that it didn't got involved in robbin' or headed west lookin' for gold," Daniel replied.

"Then the job sounds perfect for me," John said.

"Ya said you from Georgia. Whereabouts?" Daniel asked.

"Outside Atlanta."

"Damn shame what those blue devils did to that city. 'Twas a nice city, now nothin' but carpetbaggers and such. I'd never go there."

"You've been?"

"Back in '59 I visited," Daniel said.

"You said young folk don't do honest work 'cause they either head west or rob. Do you mean bank robbery?" John asked.

Daniel grew quiet.

"Did I say something wrong?" John asked.

Daniel pulled the reins hard, bringing the wagon to a full stop. "We don't talk to strangers about such things, do you hear me?"

"I'm only asking 'cause you brought it up," John said defensively.

"Best you keep to yourself and not talk about robbing or gangs; you hear me? Don't be a damn fool like my son. His big mouth got him a bullet to the brain."

"He was murdered?"

"Those James and Younger boys, they shot him 'cause they think he helped them Pinkertons. Well, he didn't, I'll say that much. My boy would never do anything to hurt any Bushwacker or Confederate. He ain't no traitor."

"I fought for the Cause," John said.

"Yeah, I know. You mentioned it in your letter. How many years?"

"Four. Most of the campaigns in the east, I fought alongside General Lee," John said.

"That damn war brought nothing but death and poverty to our part of the world. I never agreed with that tyrant Lincoln, but all that war got us was a whole lot of nothin'."

"You sound like me."

"Best you keep that opinion to yourself too."

"I will."

Daniel snapped the reins and the horse lunged forward.

"You said the James and Younger Gang killed your son? I'm sorry about that. I heard the gang was almost massacred in Minnesota."

"That's what the paper says," Daniel said.

"Say, did they return, the James brothers? Should I be watching my back?"

Once again, Daniel pulled the horse and wagon to a stop. "Boy, are you dumb or somethin'? It's fine you ask me, but you go around the area askin' that sort of question, you'll find a forty-five slug in your head."

"Understand," John answered, nodding.

Daniel snapped the reins and the horse trotted forward.

They spent the remaining time sitting in silence.

Daniel turned the wagon and headed down a long and windy drive until it ended at a small two-story white house. He stopped the horse, but before John could jump off, he grabbed his arm. "Listen here. I hired you to come help me prepare the farm to get our crop in the ground this spring, not to be asking questions. I know what them James and Younger boys did might sound exciting, but it ain't. I'll answer this once and no more. Them James boys ain't here. They abandoned the Youngers in a grove of trees outside that town. Last I heard, they headed south, some say Mexico, others Texas. I heard Tennessee, Nashville to be exact, but no one knows. Now, is that enough?"

"Yes, sir, it is," John said, hopping off the wagon. He looked around at the rolling hills of the farm. The smell of rich earth filled his nostrils. He had looked forward to working the farm while also playing detective, but his time there might be short lived. If Daniel was right, he'd be heading south, but before he could make that decision, he'd need to confirm. However, until then he'd play the farmhand and get his hands dirty like the good old days back in Georgia.

THE END

READ THE FIRST CHAPTER FROM THE NEXT INSTALLMENT OF THE WANDERER SERIES.

TORN ALLEGIANCE: BOOK 3

PROLOGUE

"I have always found that mercy bears richer fruits than strict justice." – Abraham Lincoln

TWENTY-TWO MILES SOUTH OF ST. JOSEPH, MISSOURI

NOVEMBER 17, 1876

The loud bang of the heavy door slamming shut woke John. He opened his eyes to find he was immersed in darkness. He struggled to move but quickly discovered his arms and legs were bound. *Where am I?* he asked himself. The last thing he recalled, he had been asleep when men came into his hotel room and knocked him out.

Wanting to sit up, he struggled but eventually got into a sitting position.

"Who is that?" a voice called out from the darkness.

"Garrett?" John asked, recognizing the voice.

"John, is that you?" Garrett called out from across the pitch-black room.

"I think we were double-crossed," John said.

"It appears that way," Garrett said with a sigh.

"Any idea where we are?" John asked.

Garrett looked around but, like John, saw nothing. "Wherever they have us, it's the darkest place this side of hell. Last thing I remember is looking up and seeing two men; then everything went black. Now I'm here."

"My entire body hurts, and my head is throbbing. I guess they must have done a number on me. Say, are you tied up too?"

"Yeah, like a hog," Garrett quipped.

Faint chatter hit their ears.

"Who is that?" John asked.

"Ssh," Garrett said, hoping to hear who it could be and what they were saying.

The voices grew louder until they almost sounded as if they were in the room. The sound of keys followed by the clack of a heavy dead bolt told them, whoever it was, they were coming inside.

The door creaked open. A faint glow washed over John and Garrett. Standing in the open doorway were two shadowy figures. One quickly entered the room, grabbed Garrett by the arm, and pulled him to his feet. In a raspy voice the man said to his compatriot, "Get the other one."

"My feet," Garrett said.

The man pulled a knife and cut the bindings around Garrett's ankles.

The second shadowy figure came in, marched over to John, and stood above him. "Get up."

"If you'll give me a minute, I'll do just that," John

said, straining to rise.

Impatient, the man took John by the arm and forcibly brought him to his aching feet.

"I can't walk," John said.

Like the other man, he bent down and cut John's bindings. "There, now move," he said and shoved John forward.

"Where are we going?" John asked.

"Just keep your mouth shut," the man barked.

John exited the room. The dim light took a second to adjust to, but when he did, he saw he was inside a barn. All around him stakes of tobacco hung drying, and the rich but pungent smell of the leaves overwhelmed his senses. At the far end John spotted Garrett sitting in a chair. Next to him stood a man, and next to him another chair sat, no doubt one he'd be sitting in.

The man pushed John along until he was in front of the chair. "Sit down."

John turned and plopped down in the chair.

The two men stepped aside.

John took a moment to look around and get his bearings. He didn't recognize the barn and had no idea where he was. Several oil lanterns lit the space, casting their orange light across the barn. He tried to spot anyone else but couldn't.

A door opened behind them.

Curiosity begged John to turn around and see who was coming, but fear of getting struck curtailed the desire.

Two men appeared to the side of John. They whispered something unintelligible then separated, with one taking a chair and placing it feet from John and Garrett. He was middle-aged and had a thick beard and deep-set eyes. His physical stature was average, and his attire told them he was a man of some means.

The second newcomer stepped past the seated man and leaned against a support beam. He pulled out a cigar, struck a match, and lit his cigar, puffing several times until the end glowed bright orange and thick puffs of smoke billowed all around him. He blew out the match, tossed it on the dirt floor, and stomped it with his boot.

"Who are you?" Garrett asked the seated man.

The man leaned back and replied, "Funny, I'm here to ask you the same question."

"I think you know who I am, so why not tell me who you are," Garrett said defiantly.

The man chuckled and said, "You're right. I know who you both are and what you are. I just wanted to see what you'd say."

Garrett leaned forward and squinted. His eyes widened when it dawned on him who it was he was talking to. "Wait a minute, you're Frank James."

The man turned around and looked at the smoking man behind him.

The smoking man nodded as he took a long inhale of his cigar.

Facing Garrett once more, the man said, "You're right. I am Frank James, and the man behind me is my brother Jesse. We heard you were sent to find us. Well, you have, but I can tell you this one simple fact. Soon, you'll regret you ever did."

"Are you planning on killing us?" Garrett asked.

Jesse stepped from the shadows and walked up next to Frank. He removed the cigar from his lips, looked at Garrett carefully, and answered, "One of you will die for sure; the other, well, you're going to help us with some critical information."

"What sort of information?" Garrett sneered.

"There's a train coming in from Denver, arriving in a couple of days. Word is it's loaded with something valuable."

"We don't know what you're talking about," Garrett said.

John watched the exchange and had a distinct feeling that if Garrett didn't shut up, he'd end up with a bullet in his head. Hoping he could negotiate, John said, "How about you let us *both* go?"

"Now, you see, that's not going to happen. We need to send a message to your boss back in Chicago, and the best way to do that is by sending him parts of one of his men," Jesse said.

"What sort of information are you looking for?" John asked.

Garrett shot John a look and barked, "You don't negotiate with people like this."

"I'm trying to keep both of us alive," John said.

"By striking a deal with criminals?" Garrett asked.

"I believe these men can be bargained with. Hell, everyone has a price," John said.

Jesse stepped forward and said, "There is no deal. We're already aware of the train; we just need to know what's on it."

"I won't tell you anything," Garrett said defiantly.

"If you keep us both alive, I'll tell you what's on the train, and I'll sweeten the pot with some information you'll definitely need," John said.

"Don't you dare make a deal with them." Garrett seethed with anger at John.

John ignored Garrett and asked, "Do we have a deal?"

Frank and Jesse looked at each other.

Jesse stepped forward and asked, "Not sure, what's on the train?"

"A carload full of United States Treasury notes."

"What in the hell would we do with new notes? They'll be able to track them," Jesse said.

"No, these are all previously issued notes. They're coming from the treasury in Denver and headed to Washington, DC. It's to do with the Resumption Act; they're to be destroyed," John explained then added his sweetener. "But I can understand your concern, so I can connect you with a man in Texas who can help you rid yourself of them in exchange for gold coin."

"What does he do with the notes?" Jesse asked, curious.

"Does it matter?" John asked.

"Humor me," Jesse said.

"He takes them to Mexico and other parts south and exchanges them for foreign currency. It's some sort of exchange-rate scam. I met the man who runs this racket a couple of years ago. He helped me track down someone.

He's a good man to know," John confessed.

"Interesting," Jesse said then tapped Frank on the shoulder and signaled for them to step away.

Frank got up, and the two walked to the far corner of the barn.

"What the hell are you doing?" Garrett asked.

"Stalling for time. Now play along," John replied.

Garrett cut him a look and whispered back, "You don't play games with these people."

"We either play games, or one of us is dead tonight. I'm going for games until we can figure out how to get out of here, and not in a box headed to Chicago," John said under his breath.

Jesse and Frank returned.

"You have a deal, but we're not letting either one of you go until we know what you're telling us is true," Frank said.

"Damn it, John, you can't make deals with people like them," Garrett lashed out, but this time he was going along with the ruse.

"I just did," John countered.

"These men are liars, thieves and murderers," Garrett roared.

John locked eyes with Jesse and asked, "We can trust you, right? If we give you the details of the train and where to move the notes, you'll let us go?"

"As a gentleman of Missouri, my word is my bond," Jesse replied. "As far as a matter of trust, it's you two traitors that I have a hard time trusting. How can sons of the South turn their backs on their own people and side with the Yankee occupiers?"

"The war is long over. Time to move on," Garrett replied, this time not acting.

Jesse strutted over, yanked the cigar from his mouth, and blew smoke in Garrett's face. He gritted his teeth and seethed, "The war never ended. We're just fighting it differently is all."

Garrett shook his head.

"Take this one away. Lock him back up," Jesse ordered, pointing at Garrett.

The other two men in the room grabbed Garrett and hauled him back to the room.

Jesse took a seat on the now vacant chair and said to John, "You're going to tell me everything you know about this train, and you best not be lying."

"I'm not lying," John confessed.

"There's an entire train car full of notes?" Jesse asked.

"That's what I've been told. To be clear, I don't have all the specifics, but what I don't know, I can find out from the Chicago office," John said.

"What do you think, Frank?" Jesse asked his brother.

"It could be true, but he could also be stalling. Have we ensured we got them all?" Frank asked, referencing if any other Pinkerton detectives were in the area.

"It's just me and him, no one else that I'm aware of," John said.

"I heard it's just these two," Jesse answered Frank. He turned to the other men, who had just returned from locking Garrett back up, and ordered, "Cut him loose."

He adjusted his stance and placed his hand on the back strap of his Colt.

One of the men stepped forward and cut the rope bindings holding John's arms together behind his back.

John rubbed his sore wrists, gave Jesse a look and asked, "How did you know me and my partner were Pinkertons?"

Jesse smiled and said, "Telling you isn't part of our deal."

John stood waiting for what would happen next.

"You're John Nichols, correct?" Jesse asked.

"Yes, and how do you know my…real name?"

"I won't tell you, I'll show you instead," Jesse said, motioning for John to follow him.

John did just that and exited the barn just behind Jesse. The cool air of the early evening felt good, as did the fresh air.

Jesse stopped midway to the house, took John by the arm firmly, and said, "We have ways of finding out information. We have people, loyal people, everywhere, or people ready to take a payout; so don't think you're going to lie to me without me eventually finding out."

"Mr. James, my will to live far outweighs my need to protect that train full of notes; and I'll be honest, while the war was many years ago, I still haven't forgotten what the Yankee invaders did to my wife and child."

"They killed your wife and child?" Jesse asked, genuinely curious.

"Yes, sir, they were murdered by a detachment of bummers," John replied.

"My condolences for your loss," Jesse said sincerely.

"Thank you."

"A Southern gentleman like yourself, who fought for the Confederacy and even had his wife and child murdered, turns his back on his own country, then ends up working for the very people who murdered his family. Makes no sense, nope, doesn't at all. I don't understand how some people think," Jesse said, shaking his head.

"A man needs to eat," John said.

Jesse patted his shoulder and said, "What good is nourishing your body if your soul is starved of righteousness? Now let's get inside. There's someone I want you to see."

G. MICHAEL HOPF'S LATEST APOCALYPTIC NOVEL

DRIVER 8

PROLOGUE

SHADOW MOUNTAIN LAKE, COLORADO,
UNITED STATES

"Now, kids, hydration is critical when you're out in the wilderness. So, before we head out today for our hike, drink plenty of water and, second, make sure you bring plenty with you," Kyle Grant said to the small group of children whose ages ranged from eight to twelve. Today they were heading out for the longest hike of their summer camp and Kyle didn't need anyone dropping from dehydration. "One last thing, always remember the threes. Three weeks without food, three days without water, and three minutes without air. That's how long you need of each before you...what?"

A young girl, about ten, raised her hand.

"Yes, Melody," Kyle said, pointing at her.

"Die. But is it really three days without water?"

"That's the average," he explained. "Now, go get hydrated and finish packing. Meet me at the trailhead in fifteen minutes," Kyle said.

The group of twenty-three kids and two adult counselors stood and exited the cabin.

"You're really good with the kids," Tiffany Powell, the camp director, said with a big smile. She walked over and leaned on the table where Kyle had the backpack he was using for a demonstration laid out on.

"I love it. I can't think of a better way to spend my two-week vacation," Kyle said, a broad smile gracing his rugged and square-jawed face.

"We don't get many volunteers, and those we do, don't travel over a thousand miles at their own expense," she said.

"Like I said, I love it. Taking my vacation time and spending it on the beach drinking cocktails is fun, but I find this fulfilling, I really do."

"I could go for some cocktails on the beach right about now." She laughed, standing and folding her arms. "The kids really love having you here too. I especially think they love the police stories you tell around the campfire."

"You do know I do it mainly to scare them straight," he joked. "But is it only the kids who love having me here?" he said with a wink.

"Let's keep it professional," she replied. "You know something, I also think you make them feel safe. Nothing like having a real LAPD detective as a volunteer camp counselor."

"Part-time counselor, if it paid more, I'd be here full time, believe me," he jested.

"You have a job anytime you want it," she flirted.

The door opened and a man in his late twenties stuck his head in. By the look on his face, he was scared.

"Josh, you okay? You look like someone just got eaten by a bear," Tiffany joked.

"Tiffany, hurry, something is happening back east. Something bad."

She jumped and asked, "What's happened?"

"A terror attack, something, come, hurry," Josh said and took off.

Tiffany and Kyle followed him to the main camp station building. When they entered they found a group of people huddled over the television, from left to right the group consisted of Joselyn, Andy, George, Gwen, Josh and Vivian. She pushed past until she could see the screen.

For Kyle it was easy, at six feet three, he just leaned over the group.

On the television was a large explosion followed by a mushroom cloud rising high into the sky.

"What is that? What's going on?" Tiffany asked.

"That was Boston," Joselyn, the camp's aquatics counselor, said.

"Are you serious?" Tiffany asked.

"Yes, the news is reporting cities all along the East Coast are being hit," George, the native skills instructor, answered.

"Turn it up, I can't hear," Kyle said.

"*...reports are now telling us there have been strikes on the West Coast too. It's very chaotic but it does seem like the West Coast is under attack now. Oh, wait, we have a new video feed* *coming in from a pedestrian's phone,"* the reporter said.

The screen clicked over to a wobbly video image of Los Angeles in the far distance. A bright flash then a huge mushroom cloud rising and enveloping the entire city.

"Oh my God!" Vivian, the arts and crafts counselor, cried out with tears in her eyes.

Chatter and cross talk exploded in the group.

Kyle stood in shock and watched the video clip being replayed. One second his city was there, the next second it was gone. Destroyed in the blink of an eye by a nuclear weapon.

"Denver. Has anyone heard if Denver has been hit? My mom and dad live there," Joselyn asked.

"My brother lives there too," Andy the archery instructor, said.

"We're now getting a report from our affiliate in Topeka that Kansas City has been hit. It appears what started on the East Coast then the West Coast is now happening in the Midwest," the reporter said.

"What should we do?" Josh asked.

All eyes turned to Tiffany.

Tiffany thought for a second and said, "We wait. We don't do anything drastic until we know for sure what's happening."

"But we're at war. Cities are being destroyed," Vivian wailed.

"This is not a time to panic. Our number one goal is to take care of these children. Does everyone understand?" Tiffany asked.

"I agree with Tiffany. Let me call a contact I have in

Denver," Kyle said pulling out his mobile phone. He dialed and put the phone to his ear.

The phone clicked and a message played. *"All circuits are busy. Please try your call again later."*

Kyle tried again and got the same message. He looked at Tiffany and said, "I can't get through. Can someone else try to call out?"

"I'm getting a message that says all circuits are busy," Joselyn said.

"Me too," Jacob said.

Tiffany pulled out her phone and tried, "Same here."

"Try the landline, see if that's working," Joselyn suggested.

Kyle picked up the landline phone and called the number he was trying on his mobile. He put it back on the cradle and said, "Says the circuits are busy."

"Oh no. What does that mean?" Vivian asked, her hands trembling.

"It means everyone is calling out like us, nothing more," Kyle replied, hoping to calm the situation down but feeling deep down that he had just witnessed the end of the world live on television.

"Turn up the TV. They're saying something about Europe," Vivian exclaimed.

Josh turned the volume up.

"…Paris, London, Copenhagen, Berlin—all gone. We have preliminary reports coming from our international correspondents in the Far East that Beijing, Hong Kong and other major cities and military installations in China have been hit by the United States as a retaliation for the attacks against what is now over a dozen

major US cities," the reporter said and paused as she became overwhelmed with emotion. *"I don't know how long we'll be live but I pray that when this is over..."* The feed went dead and the screen turned blue.

"Where was that news station?" Kyle asked.

"That was Denver," Tiffany said, her voice cracking a bit.

The room grew quiet save for the sound of people crying.

"The kids, they're waiting for me near the trailhead," Kyle said.

"Go get them. When they come back we need to ensure they don't hear about any of this. If you can't keep your composure, then let me know," Tiffany ordered, taking control of the situation.

"I can have them do an art project," Vivian said, wiping tears from her cheeks.

"I don't think that's a good idea. You're shaken up, take a few, go back to your cabin," Tiffany said turning to Joselyn, "How about we have them go swimming?"

"I'll be down at the beach waiting on them," Joselyn said and headed out.

Kyle was making his way to the door when Tiffany called out to him, "I'm coming with you."

He stopped and waited.

"I don't know about you, but I'm scared," Tiffany confided.

"I'd be lying if I said I wasn't a bit freaked out, but you handled it nicely in there. We need to keep our heads. Clearly the world has gone to shit and soon we're going to have to explain it to the kids."

"I know, believe me I'm already thinking about that. How do you say the world has ended to a bunch of kids without having them melt down?"

"You can't, this situation is fucked, pardon my French, but there's no easy answer. Just know I'm here to help any way I can, let me know what I can do," Kyle said.

She reached out and took his hand.

He looked and gave her a reassuring smile.

Squeezing his hand, she said, "I can't tell you how happy I am you're here."

"Tiffany! Tiffany!" Josh hollered from across the camp.

She turned and asked, "What?"

"The power, it's down. Nothing is working," Josh answered, his tone sounding stressed.

"This is a camp, right?" Kyle joked.

"Hold on, the power's back on!" Josh hollered.

"That's the backup generators. Do me a favor, turn off all nonessential items. We'll need to conserve fuel," Tiffany hollered back.

Josh gave a thumbs-up and ran off.

"You're like a badass general, calm, cool, and collected," Kyle quipped.

She winked at him and said, "It's called being the oldest of four and having a dad who was a Marine. C'mon, let's get those kids."

THREE WEEKS AFTER THE WAR

"Tiffany, wake up," Joselyn said, nudging her.

Tiffany opened her eyes and shot up. "What's wrong?"

"It's Josh, he took off, took the rest of the food and one of the trucks," Joselyn said.

"How? Who was on watch?" Tiffany asked, swinging her legs out of bed and stretching.

"It was George. I found him unconscious after showing up for my shift. He told me Josh approached him, they talked, and when he turned around, he got hit in the head. That's all he remembers."

"Where's Kyle?" Tiffany asked.

"I don't know. I don't think he returned yet from his run."

"That son of a bitch, I knew I couldn't trust that mealymouthed asshole," Tiffany said getting up and putting on a fresh shirt. "Did you get an inventory of the food?"

"Tiff, he took everything."

"Literally, everything?"

"Yes. He cleaned the shelves out. He said something to George about heading to Wisconsin to see if his family was still alive."

Headlamps from a vehicle shot through the window.

"It's Kyle," Tiffany said, racing out of her cabin.

Kyle exited a truck and could see the look of concern written all over Tiffany's face. "What happened?"

"Josh, he left and took all our food, everything," she

replied.

"Damn it. Any idea when he did this? Maybe I can track him down."

Joselyn came out and said, "Over an hour ago, he's long gone by now. George said he said something about going to Wisconsin."

"Well, that asshole will have a tough time. There's bandits on the roads now. I barely got away from some. It's not safe out there anymore. People are desperate, in need of food, fuel, you name it."

"What are we going to do?" Tiffany asked.

Kyle walked to the back of the truck, reached in and pulled out a box of potato chips. We have these."

"I think we're going to need more than a large bag of chips," Tiffany scoffed.

Kyle smiled, reached back in and pulled out a huge box and said, "There's like forty bags in here, and the warehouse I found off old Highway 8 had a stack of these same boxes all the way to the ceiling. Plus there's more, I found oatmeal, cereal, and rice; sweetheart, I think I might have found the mother lode. At least enough to keep us fed for a bit."

"These bandits, how far out did you encounter them?" Tiffany asked.

"Oh, six miles north."

"We need weapons," Tiffany said.

"Agreed," Joselyn said.

"I've been looking, nothing. The one gun store I came up on was ransacked," Kyle said. "I agree, we're going to need weapons to defend ourselves here because it's only a matter of time before someone not nice shows up."

The sounds of screaming children came from a bunkhouse.

The three took off running.

Kyle reached the bunkhouse and burst through the door to find several of the kids had their flashlights beaming on a spot in the far corner of the cabin. He looked and saw Vivian hanging by the neck. "Oh, Christ." He ran over and grabbed her lifeless body to see if there was any hope of saving her, but the second he touched her, he knew she'd been hanging for a while.

Tiffany followed by Joselyn raced into the bunkhouse. Seeing Kyle struggling with Vivian's body, Tiffany went to help while Joselyn went to care for the children.

"Why, Viv, why?" Tiffany asked.

They got her body down and laid her gently on the floor.

Joselyn had taken the kids out of the bunkhouse so it was safe to talk candidly. "Are we going to survive?" Tiffany asked.

Kyle gave her a sympathetic look and replied, "Yes. Yes, we are. I swear it."

She came over and buried her head into his chest. She looked so small next him with her five-foot-five stature.

He lifted her chin and gave her a light kiss on the lips. "I promise I won't let anyone or anything hurt you or those kids."

"Now what?" she asked.

"We bury her first, then regroup. Today is a new day. I'll head out in a few hours to continue scavenging."

"But you just returned," she said, embracing him tight.

"I need to keep looking and we need weapons."

FIVE WEEKS AFTER THE WAR

Kyle made the last turn and stopped at the main gate for the camp.

George appeared from behind a tall pine and opened it.

The two waved at each and Kyle proceeded into the camp. He had been out scavenging daily, but each day was growing more and more dangerous and he still hadn't come across any weapons. He was tired, frustrated and beginning to grow concerned. Soon the limited supplies they'd found would run out; things were getting desperate.

George had been putting his native survival skills to work, but to date he hadn't caught enough to make a dent. There were twenty-three children, same as when the bombs dropped. Not a single parent had showed up. It was beyond sad. On top of the children there were six adults left. A large number to feed with only small game animals and what few items Kyle could find. With Josh taking all the camp supplies two weeks before, he had all but written everyone off.

Kyle parked the truck but hesitated from getting out.

Bored, he turned on the radio and flipped it to the AM frequencies. He'd done this before but only found static; for some reason he thought he'd try again. He pressed the scan button and watched the numbers race up. They zoomed past seventeen hundred and started up again at five thirty only to stop at six hundred with a crackling voice coming over. He sat up and listened.

"...*this...States* *government broadcasting...Cheyenne...Air...anyone* *receiving* *this* *message...is...need of assistance...to coordinates 38.7445 degrees* *north,* *10...degrees* *west.* *To* *anyone* *listening...is* *the* *United...government...from Cheyenne Mountain...Station...*"

He jumped out of the truck and raced directly to the camp director's shack, hoping to find Tiffany.

Joselyn walked by with several children in tow.

"Where's Tiff?" he asked, running by.

"In the shack, I believe."

He sprinted up the small rise and burst through the door.

Tiffany jumped from her seat when she saw him. "You scared the hell out of me!"

"The government, come, hurry," he said excitedly, his breathing rapid.

"Government?"

"Yes, just come," he said, trying to rush her along.

She followed him back down to the truck. When they arrived, the message was still broadcasting. "Listen," he said.

She sat in the driver's seat and listened intently to the choppy broadcast. Her eyes wide with joy, she said, "We need to go to a higher point. Maybe we can get a better signal."

"Good idea, scoot over," he said.

"No, I'm driving," she said, sticking out her tongue and slamming the door.

They sped up an old firebreak that led to the top of the mountain. There they hoped the signal would be strong. As they climbed higher and higher, nothing changed. "Oh, c'mon," he groaned.

"Maybe when we get to the top. Have some faith," she said.

She exited the wooded trail and was now near the barren and rocky crest. She turned the wheel hard, crested the mountain and, like magic, the static lessened and the recorded message was clear enough to understand.

Kyle turned up the volume.

"To all listening, this is the United States government broadcasting on six hundred kilohertz from Cheyenne Mountain Air Force Station. Anyone receiving this message and is in need of assistance proceed to the coordinates 38.7445 degrees north, 104.8461 degrees west."

They both looked at each other. Tears welled up in Tiffany's eyes and a huge grin spread across Kyle's face. "Does this mean we're going to survive? Does it?" she asked.

"I don't know for sure, but I'm optimistic. We have to make a run for it."

"We have the bus, we all can fit."

"I'll bring the truck to carry supplies and gear, and we have a ton of diesel. I say we go for it."

"You sure?" she asked.

He paused, thinking for a second as the message replayed again. He smiled wide and said, "Yes."

***

"All the kids are going on the bus along with Andy and Gwen. Joselyn, you'll go with Kyle in the truck. I'll ride on the bus with the kids, and last but not least, George you'll drive the bus," Tiffany said.

"Please tell me you're not one of those endless nervous talkers who drone on for hours during long boring drives," Joselyn asked Kyle.

"I'm worse," he fired back.

"Great, thanks a lot, Tiff." Joselyn groaned as she walked off.

Those who were riding the bus loaded on except Tiffany. She walked over to Kyle, who waited by his truck. "Triple check, you have the map and route?"

"Yes," he answered.

"You have plenty of fuel. We're not stopping if we don't have to."

"Correct."

"Are you happy?"

"Yes."

"Good, me too," she said and headed back towards the bus. She stopped just before getting on and turned, "Kyle, one second."

He waited.

She ran up, leapt into his arms and gave him a firm

and passionate kiss. When she was done, she pulled away and looked deeply into his blue eyes.

"Whoa, that was awesome."

"I love you," she said.

Not expecting to hear that, he didn't know what to say, so he stood looking dumbfounded.

"It's okay if you don't feel the same way. I just wanted to tell you, that's all. Now let's get on the road."

***

Kyle could feel the heavy weight of fatigue hitting him as his head bobbed down then snapped up.

"Don't fall asleep on me," Joselyn warned.

"I'm okay."

"No, you're not. We need to pull over."

"No, no, no, we're making good time."

Joselyn picked up the small handheld radio. "Tiff, this is Joselyn. We need to change drivers."

"Okay, let's pull over on the shoulder just past that sign," Tiffany replied.

"Sounds good," Joselyn answered. She gave Kyle a look and said, "You heard her, big boy, pull over."

Kyle hated to admit it, but Joselyn was right. He pulled the truck over with the bus parking just behind him. He got out, ran around to the passenger side and got back in. Joselyn simply slid across the bench seat.

"Can you believe I've never driven this big rig?" she said putting the truck into gear.

"Now I'm scared."

"I didn't say I couldn't drive, just that I've never driven this truck. I've been working at the camp for three years and I'm finally driving it."

"Where you from?" Kyle asked, slouching deep into the seat.

"Denver."

"Sorry. Why didn't I know that?"

"Don't apologize. This whole thing sucks. I just don't understand why anyone would start a war, especially a war that destroys the world. I mean, who does that?"

"Dumb people, politicians, that's who. The same people who are now safe in their bunkers. You know, maybe we tell whatever politicians we meet at Cheyenne Mountain what we think about them," Kyle joked.

"You get their attention and I'll kick 'em in the balls." She laughed.

"God knows they all deserve a swift kick in the nuts."

"Do you think they'll have hot water?"

"I guess."

"That's one thing I miss so bad, a hot shower."

"Miss? You mean need," Kyle joked, waving his hand in front of his face.

Joselyn gave him a shit-eating grin and raised her middle finger at him. "Fu—" The windshield shattered and a single bullet struck Joselyn in the face and exited out the back of her head. Her limp body fell onto the steering wheel and jerked it hard to the left at a forty-five-degree angle. The truck tipped up on it's right tires and slammed onto it's right side then began to tumble down the road. Kyle was tossed from the truck after the second roll and hit the pavement, rolling to a stop thirty feet away. The truck smashed through a guardrail and barreled down a steep ravine.

George slammed on the brakes to avoid hitting the truck and Kyle.

The children all started to scream and cry.

"Stop the bus!" Tiffany hollered.

Several bullets slammed into the windshield, one striking George in the head, the other in the neck. He fell to the right and down the front stairs of the bus.

The children were wailing in terror.

Tiffany got behind the wheel and finished stopping the bus. With it fully stopped, she turned to face the children, who were sobbing and screaming. "Everyone out the back, now!"

Andy, who happened to be seated in the far back, got up and opened the back emergency exit only to find three strange and armed men waiting with their rifles all pointed at him.

"Don't fucking try anything," one of the men said.

"I won't, please, trust me. We're not armed. We have kids," Andy said.

"Jump out the back. That goes for all of you, out the back now. Arms up, no bullshit, and this will be your last warning, don't fucking try anything or I'll kill ya."

Andy jumped first. A second man grabbed him and forced him down on the ground.

One by one, the children all exited followed by Gwen then finally Tiffany. Like Andy, they were all made to lie face down on the road. Tiffany turned her head, giving her a clear view from under the bus to where Kyle was lying in the road. She prayed he'd wake and come save them.

Several men boarded the bus. They went from seat to seat looking for anything of value. One came to the back and called out, "Nothing on here but a few bags of fucking potato chips."

"If it's food you're looking for, we had it all in the back of the pickup truck," Tiffany said.

"Is that right?" the first man said. He gave his men a once-over and asked, "Where's Mike?"

"He's down the road in his position," one of the men replied.

"That dumbass disobeyed my order, I said shoot the fucking tires. No, he had to go and shoot the driver. Now everything we need is down at the bottom of that ravine."

"It's not all lost, Ray," one of the men said. "We've got twenty-three kids, two women and this limp wrist."

"Yeah, I suppose it's not all bad if we were fucking cannibals, you idiot," Ray snarled.

"No, you're not seeing it. Maybe we can trade them. Huh?"

Ray thought for a moment, and as if a lightbulb went off in his head, he hollered, "Load back up, boys."

"All right, you heard, get back on the bus," one of the men yelled, pointing his rifle at them.

Andy and Tiffany were the last in line.

Ray came over, gave Andy a look over and said, "Who the hell will want a pussy of a man like him?"

The other men laughed.

Andy cringed and begged for mercy, "Please don't hurt me."

Ray pulled him out of line, drew his pistol and shot Andy in the head.

Tiffany screamed, "Who are you? You fucking monsters!"

"Well, aren't you a feisty one," Ray said, rearing his arm back and smacking Tiffany hard in the face.

The hit was so hard she fell against the bus and onto the ground. She rolled over and caught a glimpse of Kyle moving. He looked up for a second, just enough for them to make eye contact. Not wanting him to suffer the same fate as Andy, she shook her head, signaling for him to stay down.

"Tyrone, toss that pretty little thing in the back. It's time to tame the wild beast," Ray said.

Doing as he was told, Tyrone picked Tiffany up and took her onto the bus.

Ray called out, "Alright, you sons of bitches. Good haul. Let's head back to the ranch and have us a party!"

The bus fired up.

Kyle tried to move, but his body was racked with pain. He slightly lifted his head as the bus drove past, the tires grinding the broken glass and debris from his truck into the pavement. He reached out with his bloody and battered arm and said, "Tiffany." Unable to stay conscious, he drifted off.

***

"Who is he, Dad?" a young boy asked.

"I don't know his name, but it doesn't matter, he's a man in need," a man said towering over Kyle, who was still lying in the road. "You two, get this man into the van," the man ordered.

Two other men ran over and picked Kyle up and carried him over to a large cargo van. They laid him in the back gingerly. The boy and his father got in with him.

Kyle opened his eyes, but all he could see was two blurry figures above him. "Tiff…"

"What's he saying, Dad?" the boy asked.

"Sounds like he's calling out for someone."

The boy leaned in close and whispered, "If supplies are tight, why are we saving him? You always say the needs of the many outweigh the needs of the one."

"Son, that's a good question. I saw this man, and for some reason, I felt like he needed to be saved."

"He's another mouth to feed," the son said.

"He can have half my ration."

"I still don't understand."

"Because you're thinking with your head. I'm thinking with something else. I don't know who he is or where he came from. I don't know if he's a good man or a bad man. But something tells me we need him. I could be wrong but I'm going with my gut."

"But—"

The father held up his hand. "I know what I've told you. Let's see how this plays out. Either he'll end up being a savior for our fledgling group, or he'll be the one that will put an end to it. Right now, I'm betting he's the former."

The driver jumped behind the wheel and asked, "We calling it a day?"

"Yes, take us home."

"Okay, next stop, Eagle."

CHAPTER ONE

THE WASTES (FORMLY GOLDEN, COLORADO) NINETEEN YEARS AFTER THE WAR

Kyle stared at the shadows imprinted on the concrete wall. *Who were they? Did they feel anything, or was it over in the flash of a second?* he asked himself as he reached out and touched the darkened marks. These weren't the first shadows he'd seen and they wouldn't be his last, but each time he wondered. *How could something do that?* He recalled reading the stories about Nagasaki and Hiroshima and how people's shadows there were seared onto walls and sidewalks. It was one thing to read about something, quite another to witness it with your own eyes.

A strong wind whipped past him. He turned and looked out on the barren and dead landscape. In all directions, for as far as the eye could see, a once great forest lay flattened, its trees lay like blackened matchsticks. What had taken nature generations to grow, man had destroyed in a matter of seconds.

Kyle enjoyed his solo runs into the Wastes, it was always dangerous, but there he could find peace amongst the remnants of war. Today marked the farthest he'd ventured in the Wastes, in fact, he had the record now and would no doubt hold it for some time, as the other drivers didn't like the runs here and knew Kyle was always available to take theirs if they didn't want to go. They preferred to stay on relatively easy terrain, avoiding any area near where a major city once stood.

He stepped onto the shattered foundation of the house. His eyes darted around until he spotted what he was looking for…a stairway that led to a basement. Other drivers often overlooked basements. Not Kyle. They tended to be undisturbed treasure troves for scavenging. A pile of debris, mostly the charred remains of the house, blocked the stairway. Methodically, he pulled one piece after another out of the way, being careful not to puncture or tear a hole in his hazmat suit. Patience was his friend and thankfully he had it. In the Wastes, one moved and acted differently. Rushing often led to mistakes, and in this environment, mistakes could be fatal.

Once the stairway was free and clear, he proceeded down only to stop at the bottom. A large metal fire door stood in his way. He reached down and turned the knob. Fortunately for him, it was unlocked. He turned the knob and pushed the door but it didn't open. He put his weight against it and shoved.

The door cracked, followed by a gush of air. That signaled to him this room hadn't been accessed in years, maybe even since the day the war started. Kyle stepped back. He pulled out a flashlight and pushed the door fully open. He shone the light across the room before entering and confirming what he surmised, no one had been down here for a very long time. The room was a snapshot out of time, all preserved under a thick layer of dust. Deciding it was safe, he entered.

His first observation of the basement was that it had been used as living space. In the far corner to his right, a sectional couch sat. On the wall in front of it hung a fifty-inch flat-screen television. To the right of that he spotted a pool table.

He cast the beam to the left. There he spotted a washer and dryer with clothes still dangling from a clothesline that spanned from a large support beam to the wall.

Kyle beelined it for the washer and dryer. He grabbed a large basket and began to pile in the bleach and detergents. He paused just before pulling the clothes off the line.

"Let's make sure you're clean," he said out loud. From a utility belt, he removed the wand from his Geiger counter, flipped on the device and waved it just an inch above the fabric. "Hmm, no discernable radiation. Excellent." Happily, he pulled every stitch of clothing from the line and placed it in the basket.

Next to the washer, a large metal storage cabinet teased him. He opened the doors to find a mother lode. Batteries, lightbulbs, towels, paper towels and, one of the most coveted items, toilet paper. He emptied the cabinet, leaving only a small box of fingernail polish. Just before walking away, he stopped, turned back around and took the box of polish. He shoved it into the basket.

After inspecting the left side, he went to the right. The first thing he did was remove the batteries from the remote controls.

He opened a small media console but found nothing of value.

In his excitement, he had started to work up a sweat as beads began to form on his forehead. Outside of tearing your suit, nothing was worse than your visor steaming over and making it impossible to see. He glanced at his watch. Two hours until nightfall. He had lost track of time. He'd never make it back to the eastern boundary of the Collective and he wasn't about to take the chance driving at night.

With no urgency to leave, he decided to camp in the basement and leave first thing in the morning. He stepped back and plopped down on the couch.

A cloud of dust rose around him.

On the coffee table, he saw a stack of magazines. He picked the top one up, a copy of *Women's Health*, and dusted it off. He chuckled as he read the cover: *LOSE TEN FOR THAT HOT SUMMER BODY.* "Losing ten isn't quite the problem it was back then." He laughed. *TRY THE GLUTEN-FREE VEGAN LIFESTYLE FOR A HEALTHIER YOU!* He burst out laughing because after the bombs dropped, he hadn't met one person who was gluten intolerant or vegan.

Taking a needed break to cool down, he skimmed

through the magazine, his thick rubber gloves sticking and tearing the fragile pages. Losing interest, he tossed it aside. He leaned back and exhaled deeply. Curious as to what lay farther back in the dark reaches of the basement, he aimed his light in that direction.

The light scattered the murkiness.

He slowly traced the back area, stopping when he saw something. He got up and walked over.

There, lying on the floor in a circle, were the skeletal remains of four people. Once more he asked himself who they might be.

Strictly by the size, two appeared to be children and two adults. *If this was a family, then whose shadows were seared into the concrete retaining wall above? Grandparents? Neighbors? Friends?*

His light settled on a thick, pink-covered book lying next to a small skeleton. He bent down, picked it up and dusted it off. *MIA'S DIARY* was written on the front. He glanced back down. "Hi, Mia. Do you mind if I read your diary? I promise I won't tell, I'm just curious what happened to you." Pausing as if expecting a response, he stood. After a moment, he turned and went back to the couch.

Getting comfortable once more, he opened the book to the date the bombs rained down, or as Number One, his leader, called it the REBOOT. Number One coined the name after having spent his life as a computer programmer. He'd preach that the Reboot was a good thing for humanity, which always resulted in Kyle rolling his eyes. *How could the death of billions be a good thing?*

Kyle found the page he was looking for and read.

August 19. I should be getting ready to go to the movies, but instead, I'm stuck in the basement with my annoying sister and my parents. Someone on the television just said that bombs, nuclear bombs, have landed back east. Dad says we will be fine. That Denver isn't really a target. I admit I'm scared, but I'm also irritated. Does this mean I'll miss the End of Summer Dance? I can't. Today was the day I was going to ask Hudson. Why is this happening? I hate my life.

Kyle looked over and flashed the light on Mia. "Sorry you missed your dance." He frowned and continued reading.

Mom is freaking out and Dad won't stop pacing. I hope Nana and Papa get here soon. Dad was able to reach them, but now the phones don't work, even my texts have stopped. My sister is crying. I feel bad for her…a little.

The television just stopped working and the power went out. I'm using the light coming from the window to see. I'm officially scared. What is going on?

Kyle paused and said, "The end of the world, sweetheart, the end of the world."

A bright flash just lit the basement. Mom is sitting next to me holding Olivia, she won't stop crying. The ground is rumbling, shak…

Needing to know what she looked like, Kyle skimmed through the book to find a photo. Nothing. The invention of the smartphone made it easier to take pictures, but no one seemed to print them. An entire generation's worth of photographic history was essentially lost because of the Reboot.

August 21. I don't know why I'm writing in this. No one will ever read it. Dad keeps saying we will be fine, but Mom says otherwise. After the rumbling two days ago, Dad went to go see what happened. He came back right away. Says the house is gone. Knocked down. He says the basement saved our lives. The only window in the back was cracked but didn't shatter. Dad says all we need to do is wait, that the police or firemen will come soon to help.

Kyle shook his head and thought, *How sad.*

August 25. Olivia died last night. The rest of us are sick. Dad keeps saying that soon the police or government will come to help. He and Mom argue all the time. I know Dad is lying. He just doesn't want us to be worried. I'm scared. I don't want to die. Why did this happen?

Kyle flipped the page. It was blank, he flipped to another only to find it blank as well. He thumbed the remaining pages of the diary. Nothing. August 25 was her last entry. *She must have died right after, no doubt from radiation poisoning,* he thought.

He put the book on the coffee table and looked over at the family. "I'm sorry this happened to you." He settled into the couch and closed his eyes. Thoughts of Mia and her family popped into his head. He imagined the dad, scared for his family but helpless. For a parent that most certainly had to be the worst emotion to have. As he dove deeper into thought, he slipped off into sleep.

***

A loud clang came from above.

Kyle opened his eyes, but he was submerged in pure

darkness. Night had come and brought with it the pitch black.

Shuffling and unintelligible chatter came from the top of the stairway.

He sat up just enough so his arm could get over the back of the couch. He then slid his hand down and removed his semiautomatic pistol from its holster. He raised and pointed it in the direction of the door.

Footfalls and more chatter came from the stairs, just beyond the door.

Whoever it was, they were coming downstairs and would soon be greeted by a volley of .45-caliber bullets. In the Wastes, one always shot before asking. For a second, he wondered if it was another driver, but quickly dashed that thought. He was the only driver willing to go out this far. This had to be Generates, a wandering band of nomadic cannibals who lived on the outskirts of the habitable zones. They were hellish to look at, but one should never mistake their appearance for abilities. Their name was derived from the word degenerate and over time they came to be known simply as Generates.

The doorknob jiggled.

Kyle held the pistol steady.

The door flew open.

Not hesitating, Kyle squeezed the trigger rapidly.

A scream came, followed by the distinct sound of something heavy falling to the floor.

Kyle paused.

The patter of feet and yelling reverberated from the stairs, but the sounds were growing faint. Whoever it was, they were fleeing.

Kyle stood, turned on his flashlight and directed the beam towards the open doorway. There he saw a boy lying in a small pool of blood. He raced over, stopping more than an arm's length away.

The boy, no older than fifteen, lifted his head and groaned, "Help me."

Kyle looked at him and shook his head. He was amazed that Generates would venture this far into the Wastes and without any form of protection from the radiation that still lingered. "Idiots."

The boy reached out with a quivering hand. "Help, please."

Kyle cocked his head and for a moment considered helping but stopped when he saw the necklace the boy was wearing. "Who ever imagined ears would be a fashion statement?" The boy's necklace was nothing more than a thick piece of twine but what hung on it gave a clear picture of Generates and their habits. A single ear was taken as a trophy from every human a Generate would kill. Kyle knelt down and said, "If I just look at you without knowing anything about your kind, I see a teenage boy. A boy crying for help, needy, and scared."

The boy coughed heavily and spit out a considerable amount of blood. "Please."

"I count, um, four ears. Wow, you've killed four people, good for you. Tell me, do you throw parties when you hit a certain number?" Kyle mocked.

Coughing louder, the boy cried, "Help."

"You know something, I will help," Kyle said,

reaching out and dragging the boy close. He cradled the boy's head in his lap, placed one hand under his chin and the other on the top of his head. "There are two different types of help. There's helping someone else and there's helping yourself. I'm gonna help myself, as I know your people will be back soon and in greater numbers," he said and twisted hard, snapping the boy's neck. Showing disdain, he tossed the boy's lifeless body onto the floor and stood. He got up, grabbed the basket and raced up the stairs towards his truck.

The first thing he did when he reached the truck was open the hood and reconnect the battery and the two spark plugs he always removed when parking overnight. It was a small precaution he took so no one would steal his truck. Without a truck, he couldn't be a driver, and if he wasn't a driver, he wouldn't be able to support himself and his wife, Portia. It could be said that his truck, a 2016 Ford-150 Raptor, was his lifeblood, because it was.

Driving at night was something he tried to never do, but he had no choice. He fired up the 3.5-liter, V-6 engine, put it in drive and slammed on the accelerator. The tires spun, spit rocks, then gripped the surface and lunged forward. He pulled the wheel hard, turned left and exited the driveway.

"Driver Eight, come in. Over," the radio crackled.

Shocked that his truck-mounted ham radio worked this far out, he hesitated to pick it up.

"Driver Eight, come in. Over."

He took the hand mike and replied, "Go for Driver Eight."

"Where the hell have you been?" a man barked.

"Doing my job. I'm out of area, you know that," Kyle answered.

"We've been trying to reach you for over six hours."

Annoyed, Kyle asked, "Is there a reason you're radioing me?"

Silence.

"Well?" Kyle asked.

"It's Number Two, he's missing. He was with Driver Ten."

"You do know I'm in the Wastes near Denver? I'm a solid three-day drive away."

No reply.

"You there?" Kyle asked.

"We think…" the man said before another voice came on the radio. *"This is Number One. My son is missing. I'm ordering you to go to look for him."*

"Sir, I'm in the Wastes, nowhere near Driver Ten's route, which was west towards—" Kyle said but was interrupted.

"They're somewhere in Salina," Number One said.

"Salina, like Rocky Mountain Republic, Salina?" Kyle asked.

"Yes."

"They're in Rocky Mountain Republic territory? Why would they go there?" Kyle asked confused.

"Pay no matter," Number one said.

"Like I said, I'm a good three to four days' drive from there," Kyle said.

"Go find him," Number One ordered.

"Sir, hasn't he done this before?" Kyle asked. It was

true, Number Two had disappeared other times, only to pop up a day or so later. This must be different, so Kyle pressed. "How long has he been gone?"

"Three days out of contact," One said.

"Can you tell me why they were going there? It might help."

"No, I can't, but you know Two, he does these sort of things, but I fear he might have gotten himself into some trouble this time," Number One said.

"Nothing, sir? A clue might help me."

"Driver Eight, how long you been driving for me and the Collective?"

It was an odd question. In fact, merely having a conversation with Number One was odd. "Eighteen years now," Kyle answered.

"If you'll remember, I found you lying on the side of the road half dead."

"I remember," Kyle said, his thoughts going back to that day many years ago. It was a day he'd never forget and the reason he ended up becoming a driver.

"I've been good to you and your wife. Be good to me. Consider this a personal favor," Number One beseeched.

"Fair enough."

"And, Driver Eight?" Number One said, his tone becoming steely.

"Yes."

"Don't come back empty-handed."

CONTINUE READING EXCLUSIVELY ON AMAZON

ABOUT THE AUTHOR

G. Michael Hopf is the best-selling author of THE NEW WORLD series and other apocalyptic novels. He spent two decades living a life of adventure before he settled down and became a novelist full time. He is a combat veteran of the Marine Corps and a former executive protection agent. He lives with his family in San Diego, CA

Please feel free to contact him at geoff@gmichaelhopf.com with any questions or comments.

www.gmichaelhopf.com

www.facebook.com/gmichaelhopf

G. MICHAEL HOPF

Books by G. MICHAEL HOPF

THE NEW WORLD SERIES

THE END
THE LONG ROAD
SANCTUARY
THE LINE OF DEPARTURE
BLOOD, SWEAT & TEARS
THE RAZOR'S EDGE
THOSE WHO REMAIN

NEW WORLD SERIES SPIN OFFS

NEMESIS: INCEPTION
EXIT

THE WANDERER SERIES

VENGEANCE ROAD
BLOOD GOLD
TORN ALLEGIANCE

ADDITIONAL BOOKS

HOPE (CO-AUTHORED W/ A. AMERICAN)
DAY OF RECKONING
MOTHER (EXTINCTION CYCLE SERIES)
DETACHMENT (PERSEID COLLAPSE SERIES)
DRIVER 8: A POST-APOCALYPTIC NOVEL

BLOOD GOLD

CPSIA information can be obtained
at www.ICGtesting.com
Printed in the USA
LVHW031607280319
612190LV00001B/71/P

9 781986 902137